THE CALUM - 10TH ANNIVERSARY EDITION

XIO AXELROD

The Calum - 10th Anniversary Edition

Calum, The - 10th Anniversary Edition / Xio Axelrod. -- 1st ed.

I can't believe The Calum is ten years old! That means it's been ten years since I first hit publish and officially kicked off this crazy second (third?) career of mine.

The book's original title was The Jamie, inspired by my love for Diana Gabaldon's Outlander series. Fun fact: I actually wrote to her asking permission to use the name and references. (I have yet to hear back.) I chose the name "Calum" because, at the time, it wasn't one I'd seen in the books I'd read, and it sounds pretty cool when you say it out loud.
CAH-lum.

Of course, my Calum dislikes people calling him by his first name. He prefers "Duff."

Oddly enough, a film hit the cinemas not long after my book called The DUFF. It was not a very...er...flattering term (Google it, lol!) but I had fun trying to market the book against the film's campaign.

When I first released the novella in December 2014, I kept it quiet as sort of an experiment. I was dipping my toes in the publishing waters. But if you know anything about romance authors, you know they're a supportive bunch. As soon as my network learned I'd written a book, they offered to share it in their newsletters and on their social media platforms. Pretty soon, it was everywhere!

It was an overwhelming experience, like going from zero to sixty in no time at all. I haven't looked back since.

In those early days, I was part of a writing community that came together once a year to network, celebrate, and learn. I miss that, and I hope we can find something like that again. I'm thankful for the many authors who have supported me over the last decade, and I'm honoured to call so many of them my friends.

I must give a special shout-out to Denny S. Bryce and Dena Heilik for pushing me to publish back when you could only find my scribbles on Tumblr.

My heartfelt thanks go to Susan Scott Shelley, Robin Covington, Avery Flynn, Kimberly Kincaid, Laura Kaye, S.C. Mitchell, Beverly Jenkins, Kristan Higgins, Alethea Kontis, Grace Burrowes, Pintip Dunn, Kate Quinn, Eloisa James, Liz Berry, Jillian Greenfield Stein, Connor Peterson, Gene Doucette, Tracey Livesay, Leslye Penelope, Veronica Forand, and Kim Golden for all the early encouragement.

So many talented, kind, and generous authors have helped shine a light on my work. I am grateful to Asa Maria Bradley, Reese Ryan, Karen Rose, Christina Lauren, Farrah Rochon, Casey McQuiston, Jennifer L. Armentrout, Angel Payne, Helena Hunting, Kwana Jackson, Roan Parrish, Priscilla Oliveras, Carrie Ann Ryan, Sonali Dev, Audrey Carlan, Katee Robert, Sierra Simone, Kristen Callihan, Sarina Bowen, Colleen Hoover, E.L. James, Mia Heintzelman, Lucy Score, Kennedy Ryan, J.R. Ward, Tia Williams, Tessa Bailey, Alyssa Cole, Christopher Rice, and Rebecca Yarros for championing my writing over the years and for reminding me that I belong in this space.

I'm definitely forgetting some names, and I'm sorry! Just know that if you have ever shared a post, given me a boost on your platform, or sent me a note of encouragement, I am eternally grateful for every bit of it. Storytelling is my lifeblood. I once thought songwriting was my only tool to facilitate the ideas in my head. I stand corrected thanks to my incredible readers (I have THE best ones. Fight me, haha!) author, and industry friends. I hope you all stick around for the next ten years. I have some really fun things on my to-do list. 🙂

Be kind to each other, defend and protect human rights for all, and remember to support your local bookstores and libraries.

Keep Calm and Calum On!
~Xio

Dedicated to Lou Harper who designed one of the early covers for the Calum, as well as the cover for Calum Me Maybe.

Also dedicated to M.J. Rose who was a kind, talented soul with a vision as big as the sky.

May they both rest in peace.

This is also for the sassenachs.

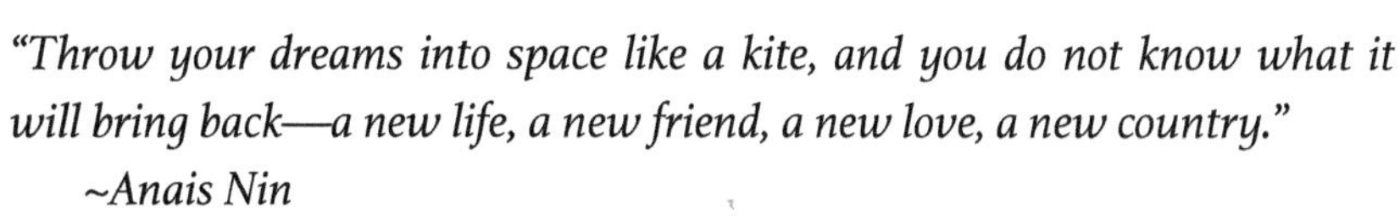

"Throw your dreams into space like a kite, and you do not know what it will bring back—a new life, a new friend, a new love, a new country."
~Anais Nin

1

A SOUND PLAN

Lovie Grant wished like hell that she had paid the five dollars for the airline headphones.

But that balloon had popped, and now she was stuck listening – again – to Joana's latest "brilliant" plan. She hunched her shoulders and buried her face in the in-flight magazine.

Anything to avoid one more word about their freaking trip.

"Are you even listening to me?" Her shrill tone bounced off the airplane window and directly into the oh-my-God-let-me-off-this-sky-bus-before-I-kill-her section of Lovie's brain.

"What is it now, Jo?"

You're not paying attention. And you keep sighing like you've been left home on prom night."

"I'm just tired, and I can't sleep on planes." *And I should be relaxing on a beach instead of chasing after you.*

Flip. Flip. Flip.

Page after page taunted her with one photo of crystal blue waters and palm trees after another. There would be no palm trees where they were headed.

Which asshole decided to put that magazine in her seat-back pocket?

"You're upset."

How very astute. "It's a scientific fact that a lack of sleep causes a decrease in the neurotransmitters that regulate mood." Flip. "Otherwise, I'm fine, Jo. Let it go."

"I call bull. You've already convinced yourself that this is going to suck." Jo's bottom lip poked out in her signature pout. The picture of a bratty twelve-year-old was nearly complete with her blonde locks twisted into two braids and her bright pink Juicy sweatpants.

Lovie's best friend, roommate, and constant damsel-in-distress had a plan. A good plan, she'd said. A sound plan if you dared to believe her. Lovie didn't, but the plan was this:

Go to Scotland
    Find "The Calum"
    Marry him

Jo had been saving up for this particular trip for three years – ever since Lovie picked up a dog-eared copy of *A Laird to Love* at a used book store. It was a great read, sure, but why the hell did *that* one have to fall out of the stack?

Like millions of other women around the globe, Jo had fallen in love with its hero, Calum MacKenzie.

Unlike most of those other women, Jo believed someone like him was just across the ocean, waiting for her.

"The Calum," Jo explained to anyone who stopped long enough to listen, was the perfect man. A lover and a fighter, he was a chivalrous, six-foot-four redhead with a six-pack and a penchant for languages. You could find variations of him in the pages of Jo's vast collection of romance novels.

. Covington. Cage. Colton.

She had shelves filled with ideal men, but The Calum somehow stood out from the rest. Enough to convince Jo that she needed to go to Scotland and find him.

Each year since college, they'd flipped a coin to see who would pick their Christmas vacation destination. This year, Lovie lost. So there they were, thirty-five thousand feet above the Atlantic, on their way from Philadelphia to Brigadoon...er...Inverness.

Lovie couldn't believe she'd agreed to spend her measly handful of vacation days tailing Jo through the Scottish Highlands. It was going to be cold and damp.

And damp.

And fucking cold.

There was a beach somewhere with her name on it, and that name was getting washed out to sea. Or sat upon by German tourists. Her lungs deflated in a heavy sigh as her dream of endless mojitos drifted away on the clouds below.

"You didn't have to come with me, you know."

Yeah right. Lovie laughed. "You get lost in Chinatown. I can't even imagine you on your own in another country. Of course, I had to come with you."

"Your confidence is inspiring," Jo deadpanned. "I am perfectly capable of looking after myself." She drew her tiny feet into the seat and hugged her knees to her chest. "I don't need a babysitter."

"Okay, how about a bodyguard?"

Jo snorted. "You're not much of one."

Lovie turned, her brow arched. "I've got four inches and twenty-five pounds on you. Put on your seatbelt."

"Yes, *Mom*," Jo said as she fumbled with it. "I've got it all worked out. When I meet The Calum, and I will meet him, I'll just play it cool and casual. Like I'm not into him at all. Show just enough of the girls to make him pant after me." Jo smacked the metal ends together like she was trying to force a size ten foot into a size six shoe. "What's wrong with this thing?"

"Oh, for the love of..." Lovie reached over and untwisted the contraption, closing it with a snap.

"I had it."

"Sure."

"Anyway, as I was saying, I'll be like a piece of candy that he can't wait to unwrap." Throwing her blonde locks over her shoulder, she batted her eyelashes in demonstration.

"So your plan is to lustrate him until he falls in love with you?"

"Good word, *lustrate*." Jo grinned. "I'll have him eating out of my hand. You'll see."

YEP, Scotland was freaking cold. Colder than the blood of a Bond villain, but there was no denying the beauty. Even in winter, Scotland shone like a jewel. There were shades of color Lovie couldn't even name.

After a short layover in Manchester, they'd boarded the smallest plane she'd ever seen. It didn't look like it could get off the ground, much less make the – thankfully - short flight to Inverness. A taxi dropped them off at a hotel so steeped in quaint-but-quirky that it could have been a set from a Wes Anderson film. There, they were greeted with a cup of tea and some kind of oat cookies. Tasty, but ultimately unsatisfying.

One deliciously hot shower and a change of clothes later, she was a new woman. A starving woman. The weather wasn't awful, as long as you didn't mind a few raindrops, so they decided to walk a bit and find a place to eat.

"What did I tell you?" Jo ran into the middle of the road and spun in a Mary Tyler Moore-esque circle. She might have been better off just shouting "tourist" at the top of her lungs. "I can practically smell the history."

"I think what you smell is that pub. Get out of the street before someone runs you over."

"Pubs have history too." Jo floated back to the sidewalk, a dreamy smile on her face.

"I bet this one is older than our apartment building."

MacKinnon's Pub sat on the river in the picturesque heart of Inverness. Lovie spied a castle on the hill across the way and made a mental note to double-check their itinerary. She loved these historical towns and didn't want to miss a thing.

According to the gold-lettered signage above their heads, MacKinnon's was also two doors down from some renowned kilt-maker or other. Jo screamed with delight when she saw it.

"Oh my God, it's fate! We have to go."

"Why? Do you expect Calum will be inside getting fitted for a new kilt?"

"Shut up," Jo laughed. "He might be."

Lovie rolled her eyes but smiled. "You really are delusional."

"Yeah, well, you are a humbug."

"What I am is starving." A peek at the specials in the pub window had her thinking twice. "What the heck are Scotch eggs? Do they have different chickens over here?"

Jo grabbed Lovie by the elbow, pulling her toward the door. "Maybe they're just super patriotic about their chickens. Let's go inside. I wanna get warm, get a bite, and get some hot guy to talk Calum to me."

"Fine, fine. Let's eat and scout the locals." Hopefully, they'd have some Scotch bacon in there too. Breakfast for dinner was a vacation must.

2

—————

HOME AGAIN

C.J. MacDuff gripped the phone so hard his knuckles crunched. He strained to keep his voice calm as the man on the other end explained why he couldn't come around to patch the roof for another two weeks. In the dead of fucking winter.

"One o' my guys is down sick with flu, and the other's got a bairn due any minute. I just dinna have the man to do it."

Duff ran a rough hand over his face. "And how much would it cost to free up a man to do it sooner?"

"Well..." He pictured the wanker totting up the profit in his head. "I could call up me nephew. Have him come 'round, say...Thursday?"

"Thursday?"

"Aye, but it'll cost ye."

"Fine. Thursday." Duff pulled out his smartphone and opened his bank's mobile application to move some money around.

"Alright, then. Though why ye'd even bother with that old ruin, I'll no understand. Yer wasting yer money if yer wantin' my opinion."

"I'm no' interested in your opinion."

Undeterred, the idiot blathered on. "You know, if yer grandmother had sold the place ten years ago-"

"One thing has nothing to do with the other, and none of it is your concern. See you Thursday." He hung up. Carefully, because his instinct was to rip his Gran's phone out of the wall, but that wouldn't do.

Five roofers. He'd called five roofers and got the same bullshit story.

"Too busy."

"Canna do it 'til next week."

"...next month."

"...the end of the year."

Was it always like this? No wonder the bed-and-breakfast was operating in the red. The place would undoubtedly go under were it not for the money he sent home regularly.

It had been five years since Duff had stayed in Inverness for longer than a day or two.

Only his best friend's wedding could bring him back now. That and his grandmother, who was clearly in more dire straits than she'd let on in their weekly phone calls.

The state of the place was shocking. There were cracks in the plaster and dangerously loose floorboards, and they should have replaced the kitchen cabinets ages ago. The roof was the worst of it, sporting a gaping hole right over her bedroom. The place needed sorting out. Or burning down.

Gran would rather sell the fillings from her teeth than admit she needed help, never wanting to burden him. She was never a burden, but it meant extending the two-day trip into two weeks.

It wasn't her he'd been avoiding.

Two weeks in Inversneckie was thirteen days too long. The city of sixty-thousand made him claustrophobic, with its small-town mentality and ancient superstitions. Privacy was as foreign a concept as blue cows.

Every familiar face contained some shadow of judgment. *There goes that thievin' Gregor's boy. Like father, like son.* He could see it in their squinting eyes. Hear it in their self-righteous voices. Still, it was a chance to spend time with his gran, and he had missed her.

"Oh, darlin'! You've got this all fixed up already?" She shuffled into the kitchen, smelling of lavender and Flexitol balm. Her hand shook as she pushed her glasses to the top of her snow-capped head.

"Yeah, Gran. It's all sorted." Duff tested the hinges on the newly repaired cabinets. The fresh coat of stain on the wood was still a little tacky to the touch. "These shouldn't give ye any more trouble, but we'll give it another day to dry."

Her face lit up with such pride. It warmed and embarrassed him at the same time.

"Aren't you a dear?"

Being back at the Golden Thistle Inn was the closest thing he had to a homecoming. The place was empty these days due to its run-down state. Gran herself was getting on in years. She was still the lively, rosy-cheeked bearer of biscuits and warm milk that used to tuck him in at night, but she moved much slower now. It had become impossible for her to keep up with the B&B on her own. He needed to find permanent help for her. That, or persuade her to sell it.

"Yer such a big help to me." *When you're around.* She would never say it, never begrudge him his freedom, but guilt niggled at his conscience.

"It was nothin', Gran. I'll check on the roof, and then I'm off for a bit." He shrugged into his jacket, the well-worn leather molding to him like a second skin. "Need anything from the shops?"

"Och, no. I'm all sorted, dear. Will ye be back for tea?"

"I shouldn't think so. I'm meetin' up with the lads at the pub."

Her worried frown was slight. "Weel, you have a good time. Try an' stay outta trouble."

"Dinna fash, Gran." He kissed her warm cheek, giving her the cheeky grin she loved so much. "I always try."

"I'm stuffed." Jo sat back in the booth and rubbed her non-existent tummy.

"I've never seen you eat so much." Lovie had polished off a fair bit of food herself. It was absolutely the best food she'd ever eaten. That or she was just super hungry.

"I think Scotch eggs are addictive." Jo groaned. "I'm tempted to order more, even though I don't have room in these jeans."

"We'll walk it off tomorrow." Lovie pushed her plate away. "I figured, after the morning tour, we could hike up to-"

"Ohhhh, no." Jo waved her off. "I am not hiking anywhere. The only hiking I wanna do is my skirt."

"Eww."

"Over my head, as The Calum grabs my-"

"Okay!" Lovie had to stop her before she could go any further. The girl could go far.

Jo's satisfied grin remained as she took a sip from her pint glass. "I'm just saying."

"I'll go by myself. I'm not going to miss it because you're lazy."

"Me? Lazy?" Jo feigned outrage. "I'm the hardest working person you know."

"Hardliest working."

"Hmmph, that's not even a word."

Lovie tossed a wadded napkin her way, but a group of men settling in at the bar torpedoed her aim. "Hellooo nurse. Hottie McHottersons at six o'clock."

"What?"

Lovie leaned in. "Don't turn around, but there's a group of potentials behind you."

"Ohhhh!" Jo's eyes lit up. "Any Calums?"

"No redheads that I can see, but-" Lovie's jaw dropped to the floor.

"But what?"

She had spoken too soon. It was a bona fide Calum. In the flesh.

"But whaaat?" Jo grabbed her hand. "Can I look?"

"Uh, wait a sec." The guy had to be six-foot-five and built like a tank. His hair was a bright coppery red, and just brushed the tops of his shoulders.

"Ugh." Impatient, Jo released Lovie's hand and turned to look. Her mouth dropped open. "Oh my God, it's..."

"Yeah." Lovie couldn't believe it. He smiled, and it was as if someone had turned on the bright lights. Goodness, gracious. She was hurtled back down to earth by the loud thud of Jo's purse as it landed on the table.

"I look like shit."

"No, you don't." Joana Lindley never looked like shit. She was Barbie without the absurdly ill-proportioned body. Blonde hair, ice blue eyes, fit but curvy —any guy's dream. But her dream guy only existed in novels, or so Lovie had thought.

She kept one eye on the Calum and another on her friend, who was fixing her makeup and fluffing her hair.

"He still there?"

"Oh yes." He was the center of the group. Even from a distance, Lovie could see how the others orbited around him. He laughed. They laughed. He drank, they drank.

Definitely some introjective identification going on there. Understandably so, he was magnetic. From his deep, resonant voice to his chiseled jaw, right down to his sizable feet, it was as if he'd walked right out of the pages of *A Laird to Love*. The only thing missing was a kilt.

Apparently finished with her adjustments, Jo flashed her patented knock-em-dead smile. "I'm going to get another drink."

"Your beer is still full."

Jo poured her ale into Lovie's empty water glass. "And now it's empty."

She slid out of the booth and sauntered – literally, hand on hip and ass swinging side to side sauntered — over to the group of mostly men. It would have been comical had she not looked so freaking good doing it. Seriously, she could've given lessons.

On cue, they parted like the Red Sea, tongues hanging out like thirsty poodles. The conversation stopped immediately as Jo snaked her way to the bar, making sure to brush against her target in the process. The Calum and his buddies all checked her out and signaled one another in some silent bro-speak, probably deciding which one would take a crack at her. None of them made a move or appeared inclined to speak.

Except the Calum.

Whatever he said had Jo tittering like a schoolgirl. She turned her back and rested her elbows on the bar, putting "the girls" on prominent display. How had she squeezed her double-Ds into that sweater?

The suitor chosen, the rest of The Calum's crew slid away. The entire event took less than two minutes. It might have been a record.

After an eternity of watching them smile and flirt, Lovie was silly with boredom. Jo hadn't even brought her conquest over to meet her. A real, live Calum. He was practically a unicorn!

She needed some air.

By-passing the court of Laird Calum and soon-to-be Lady Joana, Lovie pushed through the packs of rowdy locals scattered around the pub and stepped through the swinging door into the crisp night air.

Crossing the quiet street, she leaned against the railing that overlooked the river. The water twinkled like the night sky, reflecting the lights strung in the trees along the bank. Despite the chill, there were plenty of people out strolling. An older man and woman made their way along the walkway, hand-in-arm and speaking in hushed tones. Probably an old married couple that had taken that same walk every day for fifty years.

How romantic.

Another younger couple walked toward her, crossing the bridge that spanned the river. The woman struggled with a baby on her hip and another in a stroller. The man was on the phone, completely oblivious. Typical.

The guy didn't have a clue until, suddenly, he did. He turned and took the baby from her arms, balancing his phone on his ear, and kissed her cheek. He must have mumbled a 'sorry' because the woman smiled and shook her head.

Jesus. Everywhere she looked, people were in love. Her best friend was inside with, possibly, the man of her dreams, and where was she? Out in the cold. *And whose fault is that?*

A lone figure walked toward her across the bridge.

Black leather jacket, scarf wrapped around his neck up to his ears, threadbare jeans, and motorcycle boots. His hair, an unruly shock of black waves, was being mercilessly tortured by the breeze blowing across the river. He was tall and lean. Not as tall as the Calum, but well over six feet. Head down and hands in pockets, everything about him said *fuck off.*

To her, it said *come and get it.*

He was too brooding for such an idyllic place, like a Hell's Angel at a Bar Mitzvah.

Maybe the bad-ass persona was a cover for his shy nature. Perhaps he was a beat poet.

Were there still beat poets?

Or maybe he was an anti-hero that tried hard to keep to himself but kept getting sucked into situations where he had to save the day —moving from town to town, leaving broken hearts in his wake. He wasn't one to settle down. Oh no! But deep down, he was lonely and waiting for the right woman to love him.

Lovie rolled her eyes. *I'm starting to think like Jo.*

Whatever the case, she wanted to unravel his secrets. But she was never one to approach strangers. That was Jo's gig. She pretended not to see him as he walked by her, even though the pull to solve the mystery was strong. After he had passed, she turned to get a look at the view from behind. In those jeans, it was well worth a look, especially since his fine ass was heading right into MacKinnon's. Sweet cheeks stopped and turned as he opened the door.

Wait, was he checking her out?

She whipped her head back around to face the river, grinning like a mad woman. The sounds from the pub faded, and she dared a look over her shoulder. He'd gone inside.

It seemed a little more observation was in order. At a discreet distance, of course.

3

———

THE GANG'S ALL HERE

The scene at MacKinnon's was the same as always. Gaz was on duty, pulling pints with one eye on the patrons. Old Mr. Fitzgibbons perched at the end of the bar, awaiting his evening tea of fish-n-chips, stovies, or spag bol. Liam, Roger, Burns, and the lads all sat around, laughing and toasting to nothing in particular.

It was like stepping back in time.

At the center, as always, was Hamish, bent over in conversation with a pretty blonde that Duff had never seen. Not that he knew every pretty girl in Inverness. Not anymore, anyway. He assumed she was Sofia, Hamish's bride-to-be.

A few heads turned his way, surprised looks on their faces and more than one dirty look. He'd expected those.

"Duffy! Get yer arse over here an' have a pint on me." Roger thumped Duff hard on the back as they hugged. "How are ye, ye wee teuchter?" Just how many rounds had he missed? Roger was usually the quiet one.

"Good to see you, Rog." Duff clapped him on the shoulder. "Burns, Liam." He was greeted with turned backs and a loud belch. Well, fuck 'em. He was here for his best mate.

"Hamish."

The redhead turned as if startled. "Duffy!" He jumped up and pulled him into a fierce bear hug, nearly as big as a polar himself.

"I hate that name." Duff rubbed his sore ribs and laughed, more to draw much-needed air into his lungs than anything else. "How are ya?"

"Och, fine as ever. Awright ya wee baw bag?"

Duff nodded, smiling. "Yeah, I'm good."

Hamish glanced down at the blonde and back. His eyes narrowed, and he nodded away from the group. "Talk to ye a wee second?"

"Ah...sure." Duff followed him. "Aren't you going to introduce me to yer fiancé?"

"That's the thing." Hamish rubbed the back of his neck. "That's not her. Sofia's off with her family down in Spain." Duff glanced back at the curvy blonde at the table. Come to think of it, she didn't match Sofia's description. He thought maybe she'd dyed her hair.

"Okay, so who is that?"

"Well," Hamish grinned. "Ye see, it's like this."

Shit. Duff knew that expression. Hamish was looking for a bit of play. And here he thought that he'd finally settled down.

"Are ye daft, man? Yer gettin' married in a fortnight!"

"Keep yer voice down, will ye?" Hamish pulled Duff further away from the girl.

Over his shoulder, another young woman entered the bar. Tall and leggy, with curves in all the right places, she was a stunner. It took a moment for his brain to play catch up and realize that it was the girl from outside, the one he'd caught checking out his arse. "Are ye even listenin' to me?"

"What?" Right. Hamish.

"It's just one last go, yeah? Afore I'm marched to the guillotine."

Duff rolled his eyes. So much for being an adult. "You make it sound as if yer life's over."

"Aye, it is!" Hamish exclaimed in hushed tones. "Don't get me wrong, I love my bonnie Sofia. Truly, I do, but..." He nodded toward the buxom blonde. She was prime, for sure. Hamish bit his knuckle, making a sound that Duff never wanted to hear again. "Jes' look at that!"

Christ. "Pull yerself together, man."

"But she's braw, aye?"

She was, but Duff had bad luck with blondes. One blonde, really. "Aye, that she is. If you like the type."

"What type, horny American tourist?" Hamish wiggled his eyebrows.

"Fer chrissake, man. Tell me ye don't mean to shag 'er!"

"No! No...just have a wee bit o' fun." He licked his lips, and Duff wanted to smack him one.

"It's not a fuckin' game, mate."

Just because marriage wasn't on Duff's list of things to do didn't mean that he took the institution lightly. If you were going to make a commitment like that, you'd better be prepared to stick to it. Clearly, Hamish wasn't off to a good start.

The redhead adopted a conciliatory tone. "Look, she'll be gone in a week or so. I'll send her on 'er merry way with some nice memories."

"You'll break her heart, s'what ye'll do. And Sofia's."

"Nah." Hamish waved him off. "Nothin' so serious. She jes' wants some holiday companionship."

"You better hope it's that, seeing as ye'll be saying 'I do' before too long."

"Like I said. A bit 'o fun, so...mum's the word." Hamish still eyed the blonde like a juicy steak. Duff took a deep breath and nodded. It wasn't like he could talk him out of it, and he surely didn't need the drama. Maybe he'd let it slip about the wedding during conversation. Casually. Save the poor girl a little humiliation.

As they made their way back to the group, he stopped in his tracks. The *other* new girl had joined them. If the blonde was beautiful, this one was crazy gorgeous.

Creamy skin with a generous splash of dusky tones, cheeks dotted with tiny, star-like freckles, and thick red spirals that caressed her shoulders, almost begging to be wrapped around his fist as she moaned underneath him. Her mouth was a sin all by itself, and her eyes... *fuck.*

Duff's mouth went dry.

She was friends with the horny American. Better to steer clear of both of these women and opt for the bar. At least there, he could quench one of his thirsts without worrying about the consequences.

LOVIE WATCHED the dark stranger with interest. Clearly, he was friends with the Calum, or Hamish, as he'd been introduced. Yet, he'd settled himself well away from their group and was ensconced in conversation with the bartender. He hadn't even bothered to come over and say hello.

The pub filled up as the evening wore on. A few of the guys were joined by their significant others, and the singles clumped together like bidders at an auction. Meat markets were universal. Everywhere she looked, couples were pairing off, chitchatting away. Jo and Hamish acted like old friends, soon-to-be lovers, and the rest of his group seemed content to let them be. Lovie was used to being on the fringe, but this shit was for the birds.

Forget being the third wheel. She was the ninth passenger in an eight-passenger van.

After two hours, she'd had enough. There was only so much Cookie Crunch that her phone battery could take.

"Hey Jo, don't you think we should head back? It's getting late."

"Huh?" Jo turned her head, her eyes glazed over with alcohol and lust. "Oh. No, I'm good. I'll stay for a while longer, but you don't have to wait for me." She spoke to Lovie, but her eyes were all for Hamish. *Your place or mine*, they said. The corner of his mouth quirked up in recognition.

"Dinna fash yerself, Hamish Mackay always sees a lady home." He bowed his head, and the "lady" blushed. Hamish smiled and ran a hand through his thick, red hair, ensuring his arm rested on Jo's thigh.

Corny, but smooth.

Dismissed, Lovie grabbed her coat and walked out. She got about half a block away and stopped.

"Dammit!" She couldn't leave Jo behind with some strange guy, no matter how much of a Calum he was.

She'd known this would happen. She just hadn't expected it to happen on their first friggin' day in Scotland. It was going to be a long and lonely trip.

Rather than head right back inside, she crossed the street and walked down to the river's edge. Pitch black, it lapped at its banks in near-silence. Colored spotlights lit the bordering trees, casting ghostly reflections in purple and green. Fairy lights draped around the naked branches twinkled on the surface like stars.

Lovie yawned as the jet lag kicked in hard. Even her bones were tired, but she had no choice but to go back inside and wait. Bodyguard indeed.

"No beaches here." She sighed. "I should have just gone to Punta Cana alone. Stupid romance novels." She kicked the dirt at her feet. Jo would have been fine on her own.

Maybe. "Stupid roommate and her stupid plan."

Despite the cold, anger made her blood run hot and steady. She looked around for the nearest thing to throw. Spotting a baseball-sized rock at her feet, she grabbed it and hurled it as far as it would go.

Turns out, that was about five feet and backward. The stone landed squarely in the chest of a tall, shadowy figure.

"What the?"

"Oh, shit!"

"What the hell are ye doin', woman?" The figure bent down to pick up the offending object. Lovie pushed the hair out of her eyes and got a glimpse of long, thick fingers and a mop of black waves before he stood up and stepped into the pool of light. It was Hamish's friend, the dark, aloof stranger. He had startling, aquamarine eyes and a scowl on his full lips. A scowl that was now aimed directly at her.

"I'm so sorry, it...slipped."

"Slipped?"

"I mean, I meant for it to go in the river."

Lovie was staring. He was...wow. At least Six-foot-three, with a powerful frame, and his eyes... The only word that came to mind was unearthly.

"Dinna fash yerself." The frown morphed into a smirk, revealing a dimple on his left cheek. He held out the rock as if offering a ripe piece of fruit. "I believe this belongs to you?"

"Sorry about that, um..."

"Friends call me Duff."

"Hi, Duff. I'm Lovie. Are you hurt?"

"No damage done. Lovie, is it?" The smirk turned into a full-blown Hollywood smile. Damn. It must have been something in the Highland air. These Scottish boys were dangerous. She took the rock from him, careful not to linger.

"Do ye always chuck stones about in the middle of the night, Lovie?"

He *really* knew how to say her name. "No, I was just...getting out some frustration."

"Would that be of a sexual nature, then?"

Lovie hugged her coat tighter. "What? No!" *Is it that obvious?* "W-why would you even say something like that?"

He laughed, holding up a hand in apology. "Sorry, it's...I saw the way you were looking at me min."

Her eyes dropped to his crotch before she stepped back, suddenly aware of how alone they were. "Your what?"

"Ah, my friend," he said, grinning as if he could read her mind. "Hamish."

"Ugh." As if. That guy talked about himself in the third person. All evening, Lovie had kept trying to catch Jo's eye to see if she found him as boorish as she did. Apparently not.

"Sorry." Duff laughed. "My mistake."

"I was not *looking* at Hamish." She suppressed a shiver. "I was keeping an eye on my friend Jo."

"Is Jo yer man?"

Was that a frown? "No, Jo, as in Joana. As in my best friend." She put 'best friend' in air quotes, not feeling it at that moment. "As in the person that dragged me three thousand miles away from home during the holidays, to...uh."

"To what?"

Oops. Get back in the bag, cat.

"Never mind. It's not a big deal."

"Seems it is, if yer throwing rocks at unsuspecting passersby." He sure was milking that.

"I told you I wasn't aiming at you."

"For one not aiming, you sure hit the mark." He rubbed his chest somewhat suggestively, the smirk making a return appearance. She could see why he was friends with the dolt inside. They were probably peas in a pod. Granted, it was a very sexy pod, but it's best to ignore that—lipstick on a pig and all.

"Well, you're the one sneaking around in the dark."

"Wouldn't call it sneaking. I jes' stepped out for a breather. I sure wasn't expecting to have lethal projectiles hurled at me." He winked one twinkling eye, and she bit her cheek to keep from smiling.

"Hardly lethal."

"I think you had deadly intent, missus." He ducked his head, suddenly adorable. An adorable badass. So not fair. She gave up fighting the smile but turned away. He had this sexy voodoo thing going on. Maybe Jo was under some Highland spell. *Not this girl, no way.*

"Look, I already apologized. What more do you want?" Lovie sighed and chucked the offending rock into the water.

Duff moved in front of her and bent to eye level. Even at five-foot-seven, she barely reached his shoulder. "Hey, what's wrong?"

"I'm fine."

"Sure, I can see that." He snorted. "Violent Americans." He was close now. Close enough for his heat to dull the chill of the night air. Lovie folded her arms around her body to keep from leaning into him.

Duff's voice softened. "Sometimes it helps, y'ken? Just talking and having someone listen."

A little bit of her ice melted. His gaze was comforting and full of promise—like lying on your back in a spring meadow and staring up at a cloudless sky. Lovie exhaled long and slow while she tried to reign in her reaction. She concentrated on what she knew about him so far.

Gorgeous eyes.

Kissable mouth.

She wanted to shrink herself down like Alice and run through the wonderland of his thick and wavy hair. He was friends with the shady redhead, so points were lost there. But he didn't hang out with him in the bar, so call it even. He wasn't wearing a wedding ring. Of course, she'd checked. He seemed genuinely concerned and watched her as if he were also trying to figure her out.

But Duff. What kind of name was that? And his accent. She was no expert, but it was all over the place.

"Were you born here? In Scotland, I mean?"

The question caught him off-guard. He straightened up. "Aye." He nodded over his shoulder. "In hospital across the river on Old Perth Road, though I didna always live here."

"I thought not. Your accent isn't as, um, pronounced as your friend's." Lovie could actually understand him without too much concentration. Duff chuckled, scratching his nose.

"Hamish? We've known each other since we were wee bairns."

"So, you're more like brothers then?"

"Aye, the kind yer wantin' to kill every half-second." He pulled his collar up to his ears. "It's cold out, yeah? Come back inside and get warm."

She was already getting warm, but Lovie let him lead her back inside the pub. Once inside, they found a small table away from the loudest patrons.

"Fancy a drink?" Duff shucked his jacket, revealing a long, lean physique.

"They have anything non-alcoholic at this hour?"

"Tea awright?" He rubbed his hands together. He had beautiful hands.

"Tea would be awesome, thanks." She watched him walk to the bar because nice ass. He returned quickly with a mug of tea and a pint of ale with a shot of whiskey on the side for himself.

Across the room, Hamish held court. Half of the women around him took up the rhythm of some ancient dance, pushing their boobs and asses in his direction. He eyed each bit of flesh like a wolf surveying a herd of hapless sheep.

Lovie had never seen anything like it. "Is he for real?"

Duff glanced over. He shook his head and knocked back the whiskey. "Define real."

DUFF HAD MEANT to be heading home, but when he saw the sexy redhead by the river, his libido had other ideas. She intrigued him, to say the least. It was pretty clear that she didn't want to be there. She'd watched her friend and Hamish with what Duff thought was jealousy. He was happy to be wrong. All the girls loved Hamish, but Duff wasn't about to complain about having Lovie to himself.

"So."

"So."

"Tell me about yourself." She sat back as if preparing for a lengthy tale, which he was not inclined to provide.

"Not much to know, really."

"Somehow, I doubt that." She narrowed her eyes, studying him. His jacket lay on the chair between them. She nodded at it. "For instance, where'd you get that?"

"Seriously?"

"Yeah."

He thought for a moment. "Paris. No, Berlin. Won it in a bet." He smiled as the memory crystallized. Lovie smiled with him.

"What, in a game? Like poker?"

"Not a game, really, more of a..." *Dare? Challenge?* "Contest." A friend didn't think he could get a certain brunette back to his hotel room. Best not to share that, though.

"Some prize," she said. *You have no idea.* "Vintage Lewis, isn't it?"

Duff smiled. "Aye, fifty-two Aviakit. You know yer leathers."

Lovie lowered her big brown eyes, smiling. "Seems you do too. You travel a lot?"

"Yeah. Some." Duff sat back and crossed his arms. "What about you? What's your story?"

She looked back up. "I don't have a story, but you do. So, spill it."

He ignored the prompt, hoping she'd take the hint. "Your friend... She seems more into this scene than you are."

Lovie shrugged, the movement mirrored by her eyebrows. "This isn't exactly how I hoped to spend my Christmas vacation."

"No?"

"No." She didn't elaborate, and he didn't press, wondering what a girl like her might have to keep to herself. She wasn't wearing a wedding ring. Yes, he'd checked.

"So, you said you didn't always live here? Where else have you lived?"

"You know, ye ask a lot of questions for someone who doesna like to answer them."

Her eyes sparkled. "I answer plenty if they're the right ones. And you're eluding the one I asked you. Are you hiding something?" She smiled sweetly.

Well, now, this wasn't going at all the way he'd like. She seemed more interested in interrogation than conversation. No finesse whatsoever.

He shook his head. "Americans."

"What about Americans?" Her eyebrow arched sharply.

Ah, he'd hit a nerve. Interesting. Duff sat back in his seat, wondering how many buttons he could push.

"Ye act so entitled," he stated matter-of-factly. "Always stickin' yer noses where they don't belong."

She sat back, her eyes narrowing as if she could see through him. "It's a national pastime."

"Aye, well, I suppose yer not all bad," he backtracked, taking a swallow from his pint to cover. "I mean, Bruce Willis is American an' all."

"True." Her smile didn't reach her eyes. She sat watching him, silent as a statue. It was damned unnerving. He started talking, if only to break the silence.

"I jes' couldna live there anymore. Everyone always wantin' to know everything about you." She smiled and brought her teacup to her plump lips. He was so fascinated by them that her next question caught him off-guard.

"You've lived in America?"

What? Had he said that? He shifted in his seat. "Aye...well, I've moved around. Glasgow, London and thereabouts. New York. D.C. Miami."

"I see." He could practically hear the wheels turning. "And how did you end up back in Inverness?"

"I'm only here for...a couple of weeks, and then I'll be off again." He washed the half-truth down with another gulp of ale. "Thought it would be a good time to come back. Revisit me roots and such."

"You still have family here, then?"

"Are ye writing my biography or something?" She smiled warmly, and it was a beautiful sight. It tripped up his defenses. "Aye, me grandmother still lives here."

Sitting there with Lovie was like being in a confessional. Duff wasn't sure why he couldn't stop telling her things, especially when he got next to nothing back. Something about her invited trust, and that made him nervous. The only person he trusted was his grandmother. And there were things that he'd rather not discuss with either of them.

He finished off the ale.

"What is it that you do?" Long, slender fingers brushed back her riotous red mane. She was a beauty. Fine cheekbones set in a heart-shaped face. Cat-like eyes framed with lashes so blonde they were almost white. A mouth just begging to be kissed. "For money, I mean."

Right, she'd asked him a question.

"Er, I'm a photographer." He shrugged at Lovie's raised eyebrows. "Sounds more glamorous than it is, ye ken. Mostly portraits, landscapes, and the like."

"I see."

Time to resume his enquiry. "What about you?"

"I work for a clothing designer, but in graphic design."

"Do you love it?"

"Well, I like it. I worked hard to get my position." He was amazed that she answered, even more so when she continued unprovoked. "Started as an intern, put in ridiculous hours, and got shit pay in return, but I loved the idea of getting paid to be creative." She swirled the spoon around in her cup, lost in some memory. "Hate the place, though. It's full of pretentious Stella McCartney wannabes."

"I haven't a clue who that is, sorry." Her smile brought out his.

"A designer. Anyway, love would be a strong word when it comes to my job." They sat in silence for a while, and somehow, he was content to do just that. It was odd.

Usually, at this point, he'd be paying the check and taking the girl back to his hotel room for some overnight delight.

"I thought I'd be a photographer one day," she said after a time, her eyes on Hamish and the blonde. "But we can't all live the dream."

Duff laughed at that. One man's dream could be another's nightmare. "Dreams aren't all they're cracked up to be."

He met her eyes, and she nodded. A grin tugged at her mouth, and he had an overwhelming desire to kiss her. Just lean across the table and snog her senseless. "So, uh, what brought you and your friend to Scotland?" Lovie choked on her sip of tea.

4

———

NEEDLEPOINT

ovie woke up at four A.M. And at five A.M. At six, she gave up on the dream of sleep. It would take more than one late night to rid her of the jet lag. With her luck, the adjustment wouldn't kick in until she was about to go home.

She and Jo had returned to the hotel around two A.M., escorted by Hamish and a few of his drinking buddies. Duff wasn't among them. When their little tête-à-tête was interrupted by another drunken Scot, whose name she couldn't remember, he'd called it a night.

It was just as well since he'd just asked her why she and Jo had come to Scotland. She almost told him the truth but decided it would only make her sound as delusional as her friend. Of course, the delusion might prove true if Hamish turned out to be exactly what Jo had set out to find.

Surprisingly, he'd only kissed Jo on the cheek before saying goodnight in the hotel lobby. Lovie then helped her tipsy, besotted friend up to their room, where she promptly passed out - coat and all - with a big smile on her face—no doubt dreams of her real-life Calum in her head.

Sometime during the night, Jo must have shed the coat and

crawled under the covers, where she was still—snoring like the world's smallest buzz saw. Nice for some.

Lovie threw on some sweats and went in search of coffee. After scoring a fresh pot, two mugs, and a basket of baked goods, she re-entered the room as quietly as possible. Pouring herself a cup, she sat in the window and watched the city come to life. In the distance, a clock struck seven. They needed to get a move on if they were going to make the tour bus.

"Wake up, sleepyhead." Lovie nudged Jo's inert form with her foot. "We're going to be late."

A low moan sounded from the wrong end of the bed.

What the heck?

Lovie studied the comforter-covered lumps. She'd toed her best friend in the face.

Oops.

"It's too early." The lumps rearranged themselves and emitted a scratchy moan.

"You're the one who insisted on the earliest tour." Lovie laughed as a bird's nest of honey-blonde hair emerged from the cocoon.

"Ugh." Jo swiped at the unruly strands, her eyes half-closed. "Do I smell coffee?" Lovie handed her a cup. One milk, two sugars.

"Mmm, you're too good to me."

"Don't I know it?" Lovie jumped up and went to her suitcase. "I'll hop in the shower first. Give you time to wake up."

"That'll be a long ass shower."

"Ten minutes tops, so, guzzle guzzle."

They made the bus with five minutes to spare. The weather, while not cold for

December was damp, making you feel like you were soaked to the bone. Lovie was glad to have the comfort of a tour bus between stops. The driver kept the heat cranked up, catering to the international group.

The tour covered everything from old churches to working castles and well-kept ruins. Unsurprisingly, Jo had a literary refer-ence for each location bookmarked on her Kindle. Wandering the ancient sites, Lovie could well imagine how the romanticized grandeur of such places could inspire an author. As far as Lovie was concerned, history was a nice place to visit, but she wouldn't want to live there.

"I was born in the wrong century." Jo had been particularly reluctant to leave Cawdor Castle, enchanted by its fairy tale history and manicured gardens. She was still daydreaming about life as a medieval princess when they returned to the hotel. "Just imagine it."

Lovie snorted, doing just that. "You wouldn't last a day without social media."

"If I had been born in seventeen-forty-five, I wouldn't know what that was, now would I?"

"Can't argue with that logic."

Seventeen-forty-five, my ass. Jo had been checking her phone off and on all day.

They'd just gotten back to their room when she finally got a text from Hamish. She squealed so loudly that Lovie thought she might burst a blood vessel.

Still, she couldn't help but smile. "Is that your Calum?"

"Yep." Jo beamed. "He wants to take me to lunch. Do you mind?"

Yes. "No. Not at all."

"I hate to leave you on your own." Right. But it would likely be a hell of a lot better than watching those two circle one another like hungry seals.

"I'll be fine. I may go back for some of those Scotch eggs."

"Have a couple for me."

THE CROWD at MacKinnon's was a little too rowdy for Lovie's taste. Something about "Man United!" and "fucking Liverpool!" It was over her head, so the hunt for Scotch eggs took her into uncharted territory. Downtown Inverness.

It was tiny compared to Philadelphia, but there was still a familiarity to it. According to a flyer she'd picked up at the bar, there was a

Christmas festival in a place called Bishops Palace. After a fifteen-minute walk, she entered the historic building.

Lovie gazed up at the vaulted ceilings and arched windows. The chapel and the entire Eden Court complex had been renovated recently. The warm maple tones of the woodwork sang to her. She ran her fingers over the gleaming paneling, hoping to learn its secrets. It was clear that they'd also taken great pains to restore the stonework.

Vendors and artisans lined the two-floor structure, and she wandered from one to the other. There were local examples of folk art, pottery, and textiles. If she'd had room in her suitcase, she would have spent a fortune. After sampling handmade whiskey fudge, she broke down and bought a small amount—only a pound or three. A few curious heads turned as she walked about, but the people were friendly and warm. Weaving her way through the crowd, she spotted a familiar face.

Duff was the last person she expected to see at a craft festival, yet there he was. She made her way over to him, careful not to alert him to her presence. It was like observing a gazelle in the wild.

He stood on the side, shuffling from foot to foot, checking his phone and looking not at all like someone who was there by choice. There with a girlfriend, perhaps? Not that she cared.

As she moved closer, a small, round-faced woman handed him a bag. The woman smiled before patting him on the cheek and moving on, with him trailing behind. Her salt and pepper hair framed her face in an adorable bob, one lick curling against her cheek. They reached a table covered with handmade knits. The woman passed weathered hands over the assortment, pausing occasionally to inspect a hat or a scarf. Duff's back was to her, and Lovie caught a whiff of some spicy cologne. Had he been wearing it the night before?

"Hey, Duff."

A blinding smile spread across his face when he turned around, but it disappeared just as quickly. He glanced over his shoulder at the woman, who was still perusing the goods.

"Lovie, hey. Fancy meetin' you here." He looked over her head. "You on your own?"

"Yeah." As if Jo would give up her Highland demigod to spend the day with her best friend. "Jo's with Hamish, so..."

He frowned. "Alone?"

"Well, yeah. Only room for two in the roadster." She imitated Jo's breathy declaration.

Duff's sexy mouth contorted into a so-not-sexy scowl. "Where the hell did he take her?"

O...kay... He was awfully interested in Jo's whereabouts. Maybe, like most other red-blooded men on the planet, he was hot for her, too. Lovie grit her teeth.

"How should I know? I'm not her keeper."

"How could you let 'er go off with a stranger?" He towered over her, eyes dark and angry.

Lovie's hands went to her hips. "Wait a sec, he's *your* friend."

"I know that." He ground the words out through clenched teeth. The mood swings were intense with this one.

Okay, now she was worried. She stepped closer, meeting him eye-to-chin. "Is there something about Hamish that I should know?"

He blinked, his nostrils flaring as he took a deep breath. "No."

"Then, what's the problem?"

He gawked at her like she'd asked him the square root of pi. After a moment, his mouth snapped shut. "No problem."

Oh, there was *definitely* a problem, and Lovie wanted to know what the hell it was. They glared at each other for several excruciating seconds before being interrupted by a soft voice.

"Aren't ye goin' to introduce me to yer friend, dear?" The woman pushed him aside and took Lovie's hand. Hers were as soft as cashmere. She had the same sea blue eyes, though the right one had the dull pallor of a developing cataract.

"I'm his gran, dear. You can call me Ginny. And aren't you a rare thing?"

"Gran." Duff stepped next to her. "This is Lovie. She's visitin' from the States."

"Ohh! Weel, then, weelcome. Lovie, is it? Such an interestin' name for an interestin' lass." Lovie frowned. Had he been talking to his grandmother about her? Duff's mouth gaped open like a distressed fish.

"Uh, what me gran means to say is that...it's...rare...to, eh, find a...find an American in these parts."

"Och, no! We get Yanks here all the time, dear. I just meant-"

"Gran."

"Hush, C.J." Ginny wagged a finger at her grandson, effectively shutting him up. Lovie filed that trick away for later use. "I'm just curious as to how this beauty came to be."

Oh.

Lovie's back stiffened when Ginny reached a hand up toward her hair. Strangers always seemed to feel entitled to touch it without permission.

Is that your real hair?

Do you dye it?

I've never seen a brown-skinned redhead before.

While she understood the fascination, to an extent, it always felt like an invasion of her personal space.

"May I, dear?" Ginny smiled, waiting. Just like that, the tension drained away.

Lovie nodded and leaned down a little. The woman's touch was feather-light.

"Genealogy is a hobby of mine, ye ken." She passed a gentle hand over her crown and inspected one coily lock. "Ye've some Scots in you, I think. What's yer last name, dear?"

"Uh, Grant." She'd always found it kind of boring. Maybe that's why her parents had named her Lovie. She gave a slight shrug. "Pretty common in America."

"Ah, but it's an old Scottish name, Grant is," Ginny said enthusiastically.

"Really?"

"Aye. Old Norse." She gently tucked Lovie's hair behind her ears and cupped her cheeks. It was an oddly moving gesture. "I knew ye had Scots blood. These fiery curls couldna come from anywhere else." She laughed softly. "*Beeyoutiful.*"

"Thank you, Ginny." Lovie smiled, touched by the older woman's kindness. "That's...very sweet."

"Jus' speakin' the truth, dear. Now..." She turned Lovie's hand over, studying it.

Over her head, Duff mouthed, 'I'm sorry,' pleading with his eyes for her to be patient.

Lovie was okay, though. She understood Ginny's curiosity.

"You've the loveliest skin. Like spring whea'."

"Like what?"

"Spring wheat," Duff replied, his eyes scanning her. "Golden brown." His ears reddened.

"And such adorable freckles. Some African roots as well, aye? Or West Indian, perhaps. Beautiful people." Ginny released Lovie's hand and stepped back, smiling.

"You're just lovely, dear. Just lovely. Isn't she?"

"Aye," Duff answered quietly. "She is."

Wait, he thought she was lovely? Lovie met his gaze again, and the unmistakable heat there shocked her. God, his eyes were so...blue. *Or green. No, blue.* She blinked to clear her head and turned back to Ginny, who was grinning at them both.

"So, uh, Lovie." Duff cleared his throat. "What have you been up to all day?"

"Oh, I was just doing some sightseeing."

"All on yer own, dear?" Ginny tsk-ed and took Lovie by the arm. Despite her age, her grip was firm. "We canna have that, now, can we? Ye'll walk along with us." Duff shrugged at Lovie's arched eyebrow and fell in step behind them.

They stopped at a booth filled with local watercolors. One by one, Ginny explained each piece in soft, melodic tones.

"And this here is Cawdor Castle." She ran a crooked finger over the delicate brush strokes. "It's beautiful."

"Yes, I was there this morning."

"Though, ye ought to go to Golspie and see Dunrobin Castle." Ginny pointed to another rendering. "It's my favorite. And C.J. can take ye! Couldn't you, dear?" She beamed at him, obviously doting.

"Well, Gran, I'm sure that Lovie has other—"

"O'course ye can." She smiled, patting his cheek once more. Lovie was certain she'd seen him blush that time. Grandma's boy. It was curious for a guy in a leather biker jacket who carried himself as if he were apart from the world, but it somehow made sense. She liked his grandmother.

"For now, we should have supper." Ginny took Lovie's hand. "Will ye join us fer tea, dear? My home's no so far, o'er in Westhill."

"Um."

"O'course you will. Ye need a good, home-cooked meal to warm ye."

Apparently, Ginny wasn't accustomed to hearing the word no.

DUFF'S STOMACH ached from too much food and more laughter than he'd had in ages. In addition to whipping up a spread that could've fed an army, his gran had also supplied the mealtime entertainment, providing embarrassing tales of his youth. Lovie had eaten it all up with a glow in her cheeks.

There was something enchanting about her. The way she moved, the way she spoke, it demanded his attention. He found it hard to take his eyes off of her, something that hadn't gone unnoticed.

Gran's knowing smiles had him squirming.

Lovie Grant. The girl with the guarded, beautiful brown eyes and the careful smile. She was inquisitive. Insightful. And destined to be a little lonely on this trip, what with her friend tied up in whatever Hamish was up to.

She had asked him, flat out, if there was something she should know about Hamish, and Duff had lied right to her face. What else was he supposed to do, tell her the truth? He supposed he really should, but then it was none of his business. And he had promised Hamish he wouldn't interfere. *Just a bit of holiday companionship*, he'd said. *No romance*. Right.

What if *he* wanted a bit of romance? Lovie was brilliant, funny, and bloody gorgeous. There he was, sharing a meal and a laugh, leaving Hamish to do God knows what with her best friend. What did that make him? *A MacDuff.*

Gran pinched his cheek, dropping him back into the middle of the conversation, dishing out a bit more cranachan into his dish. "An' this wee one was covered in flooeer."

"In what?" Lovie glanced at him for help.

"Flour," he said, and she smiled, warm and bright. "Gran, I canna eat any more." He ate it anyway. it always reminded hi of her, and no one made it like she did.

"Thas what I said een it, a bhobain?"

Duff chuckled. "Aye, gran, but sometimes I havta translate fer yer old Scots tongue."

He ducked the hand that swatted at his ear. "It's true!"

"Och, you." Gran laughed. The sound of it warmed him. Lovie laughed, too. Only hers had an entirely different effect. How could a laugh be so damn sexy?

He'd agreed to take his gran shopping at the festival, thinking he'd spend the rest of the evening at the pub watching footie. This was so much better. He'd deal with the guilt later.

Lovie stood and reached for a platter. "Can I help clear the table, Ginny?"

"Heavens, no! Yer a guest in ma house." Gran deftly stacked the dirty plates and nodded to him. "Me grandson can help me, and then he can show you some o' his pictures."

Duff stiffened.

The photos he carried with him were personal. There was more than a measure of him in each exposure. The rest, he sold or shot for work, but his private collection...those he only showed to a few people.

"Gran, I doubt she'd be interested in those."

"Nonsense." Gran protested with a tsk. "He takes lovely photos, dear."

"Oh, I'd love to see some." Jesus. With a smile like that, how could he say no?

"Yeah. Alright, then. I won't be a moment." Why did the thought of sharing a few photos with her make him so damned nervous?

"I'll be leaving this fine evenin' to you two young people." And now he was even more nervous. *Thanks, Gran.*

Gran shuffled toward the kitchen but turned to call out over her shoulder. "I expect ye to come 'round again afore ye head back home, Lovie dear."

"Of course." Lovie smiled sweetly. "I'd like that."

Pleased as punch, Gran disappeared into the kitchen. Duff followed behind, and soon, they had the table cleared. Despite Gran's protests, Lovie helped.

❧

LOVIE COULDN'T BELIEVE the quality of his photography. Duff had been modest when he told her he shot landscapes and portraits, but every photo had such depth and emotion. He clearly loved his work, and it showed.

Composition, perspective, and light. That's all she remembered from her one photography class, but Duff seemed to have mastered them all. He pulled out one transcendent landscape after another. The Grand Canyon, Victoria Falls, a bamboo forest in some exotic locale... The boy got around.

His portraiture was just as breathtaking. Lovie traced the lines in the face of one particular man, his skin a deep mahogany and his eyes bright and black. It was difficult to tell how old he was, but easy to see that he'd had a hard life. His hands were gnarled and twisted like an old oak tree, the knuckles painfully swollen. They seemed to tell his story.

"I took that in Sri Lanka," Duff spoke over her shoulder as she reverently placed the photo back into his portfolio. "His name is Anoop. Was...Anoop." He looked away, haunted by some old tragedy.

"What happened?"

"Floods." Duff flipped through some other prints, handing one to her. A small boy dressed in rags sat atop a gilded elephant. They were walking on the beach, and the sea stretched out behind them to infinity. The perspective was striking.

"Did you always want to be a photographer?"

Duff rubbed the back of his neck. The muscles in his arm flexed, and Lovie was momentarily distracted. "When I was naught but five or six, me ma bought me my first camera. It was love at first click."

He sifted through a stack of photos, handing her one of a fruit stand in some tropical place. She could almost smell the bananas, mangoes, and papayas.

"I spent all of me allowance on film and development. When I were fifteen, I got a job at the local photo shop after school. Learned to develop the film. How to get the most out o' the negatives."

Lovie was beginning to see him in a new light. He was every bit the bad boy she imagined, quick-tempered and moody, with an acerbic wit. Behind all that hid the soul of an artist. And he adored his grandmother.

"Your eye is incredible, Duff." He shrugged, uncomfortable with the praise. "Really."

"Ta."

Their eyes locked, the air between them charging like a defibrillator. A slow smile spread across his mouth, and her stomach did a little flip. "Give me your phone."

Lovie blinked. "Huh?"

"Yer phone." Duff held out his hand. Lovie fished it out of her pocket and handed it over.

He programmed a number into her list of contacts—his number —and then dialed himself to capture hers.

"If you, uh, find yerself without an escort again..."

Call me. He didn't say it, but Lovie heard it loud and clear. She smiled, turning away so that he couldn't see the heat rising in her cheeks.

"Thanks, I will."

"C'mon." He bumped her shoulder. Other body parts grew jealous. "It's gettin' late. I'll take ye back."

5

───────

ONE FINE DAY

It had been another sleepless night in Inverness. Lovie was really sick of being tired. She stared at the ceiling above her bed, mapping the small cracks and bumps in the plaster.

Eventually, she gave up and went to grab some coffee, returning to the room with a small pot. No pastries this time. She had to get Jo up and out for breakfast early. They had a long day planned.

A familiar bass line broke the silence as Jo's cell phone declared, "Baby's Got Back." A hand snaked out from her general location and grabbed it, pulling it under the covers.

There was a muffled 'hello,' and then she sat straight up as if she were on puppet strings.

"Hamish! Hey! No. I was just-" Jo eyed Lovie's mug. "Having coffee with Lovie." Lovie took the hint and poured her a cup. Jo accepted and mouthed a thank you.

"Today? Wow, sure. That would be fun." The bright smile that lit her face dimmed.

"Oh, well...hang on." Uh oh. Puppy dog eyes.

"What is it?" She already knew.

Jo covered the phone. "Would I be a horrible friend if I hung out with Hamish again today?"

"We were supposed to go up to Culloden today. You know. The place that *you* went on and on about?"

"I know, and I'm sorry, but..." She grinned, pointing at the phone.

At this point, they may as well have taken separate vacations. Whatever. Who was she to stand in the way of storybook romance? "Okay, fine, I can walk around town." Or maybe reach out to Duff.

"You'll have a much better time without me. I'd only drag you down."

"I said it's fine, Jo. Go grind your corn or whatever."

"Eww! It's not like that." Jo giggled. "Not yet, anyway. I'm not that kind of girl." She fluttered her eyelashes.

"Just be careful, okay? Give me his number, just in case. And keep your phone on."

"Yes, mommy." She winked, uncovering the phone. "Hamish? What time do you want to go?" Jo jumped up and headed for the shower.

Lovie pulled out her own phone and stared.

Should she or shouldn't she? He said to do it. She pulled up the last calls, and his name popped up first. Her finger hovered over the button, but she couldn't summon the courage. "I'll text," she said to no one. "That way, if he wants to, he can pretend he never got it."

Hey I'm on my own again today.

Ditched again?

Yep.

Me too. Got roofers coming this morning but I'll pick you up after lunch.

Sounds good.

Wow, okay. Duff was going to pick her up. Lovie chose not to acknowledge the butterflies in her stomach. There would be no butterflies. It wasn't a date. She was hanging out with a new friend. A mysterious new friend. A mysterious, uber-hot professional photographer friend with killer blue eyes and a body she wanted to climb like a vine.

But still, just a friend who offered to show her around.

At the insistence of his grandmother.

But he had been a little flirty.

Maybe he just felt sorry for her.

Then again, he did give her his number. He didn't have to do that, right?

He's just a good wingman.

She flopped back onto the bed.

Crap.

WHEN DUFF ARRIVED at the hotel, Lovie was strangely silent. She met him at the entrance with a quiet 'hello,' barely meeting his eyes. He ran through the events of the night before, looking for what could have caused her mood. "Everything awright?"

She frowned. "Huh? Yeah."

"Do I need to apologize for me gran?"

"What? No!" Lovie smiled. "Ginny was sweet."

"I hope she didn't offend ye." He opened the car door and waited until she was settled to close it. When he sat down behind the wheel, she turned to him.

"She made me miss my grams," Lovie said quietly. "She died when I was nine."

"Oh, I'm sorry."

Lovie shrugged, but sadness ghosted over her face. "Thanks. And no worries, your gran is awesome."

"Aye. That she is." He started the car and eased it slowly out into the road. "She's no got a mean bone in her body. Won't put up with nonsense, either. Sees everyone as equal. Raised me Ma that way, and me Ma raised me, so..."

"So, she's your mother's mom?"

"Yeah." He didn't want to get into his family history. *Well, Da's in prison, me Ma died of a broken heart, and I'm a pariah in my hometown.* Not exactly the best impression to make.

An awkward silence passed as they headed toward the motorway.

"So, ah, let's go shoot some photos. Or we could go to Dunrobin if that's what you'd prefer."

"No, I'm good with shooting." She paused. "Unless you'd rather go to the castle."

"Well, I told gran I'd take ye." Lovie gave him an odd look and began buttoning her coat with swift, angry movements.

"You can just drop me off in town. I'm not a charity case." She crossed her arms in a huff.

The hell?

"Charity? What are ye talkin' about?" Duff hit the brake, stopping them in the middle of the road.

"You're going to cause a traffic jam!"

"Do ye see any other cars?" Duff couldn't figure this woman out. One moment, she was normal, and the next, she was just so...aggravating. "What's all this about charity?"

She ducked her eyes, but not before he caught the embarrassment in them. "I-I was just saying that you don't have to feel obligated."

Ah ha. Duff resumed the drive. What on earth did she have to feel insecure about? She practically had him panting at her feet. "Gran would be the first to tell ye that gettin' me to do somethin' I don' wanna do is akin to bathing a wild cat."

Lovie rewarded him with a soft giggle, which hit him straight between the legs. She tucked her hair behind her ear, something he longed to do. It looked as soft as a patch of heather.

"Where were you planning to take pictures?"

"I was headed up to Fort George. Ye can get some great views of the sunset from there."

"Sunset? It's only one o'clock."

"Aye, but the sun sets at three-thirty today."

Duff briefly glanced over to see her checking her phone. "Waitin' for a text?"

He'd have been surprised if she didn't have someone special back in the States. Though, if she had, she would likely spend Christmas with them instead of traveling with her best friend.

"I was checking to see if Jo had been in touch."

Ah, right. "You known her long?"

"Yeah, we met in high school and went through college together. She's older than me by a year, but she's like a little sister. Always needs looking after."

He could relate. "Bit of a dreamer?"

Lovie laughed softly. "A bit. I feel kinda responsible for her."

Duff knew all about dreamers. His father had been one, always with his grand plans and lofty ideas. As a kid, he'd wanted to dream big, too. Be just like him, his hero. Until about ten years ago, when his happy family imploded, and any remnants of his childhood were blown to smithereens.

"Dreams are dangerous things," he said. "Chasin' after them can cost ye and those around ye. Cost ye dear."

"Wow." He saw her turn to him out of the corner of his eye. "That was...deep."

"Aye, well, we Scots are deep thinkers, ye ken." He added a comic level of gravitas to his voice and was rewarded by her throaty laugh.

Christ, that sound.

She settled back into her seat. "Duly noted."

Lovie ran a hand through her hair, an auburn cloud of windswept curls. Out of the corner of his eye, he watched her struggle to tame it with some kind of elastic band.

A real shame.

Duff didn't want it tamed. He liked it wild. Free. Her hair had a personality unto itself. It suited her.

They passed the twenty-minute drive in comfortable silence while Duff stole glimpses of her. He couldn't help it. Lovie was incredibly lovely. Stunningly so, yet somehow utterly unaware of her effect on him.

It made her even more appealing.

He pulled up to the fort and parked, grabbing his camera bag from the back. "Shall we?"

6

———————

CRUMBLING WALLS

Okay, Scotland was officially fucking gorgeous. Lovie couldn't quite believe it was real.

The ground was covered in a vibrant green carpet, frosted with snow in patches.

The fort stood at the mouth of Moray Firth. The brochure explained that it had been constructed after the last Jacobite uprising when the Highland clans fought their final battles against the English. It had been used as a garrison ever since, overseeing sea access to Inverness eleven miles away.

Jo would have loved this place. Maybe Hamish had taken her there. Who knew? Lovie hadn't heard a peep from her all day.

Lovie snapped as many photos as possible, kicking herself for not bringing her big camera. Her little point-and-shoot had decent quality, but she suffered from serious lens envy when Duff unpacked his Canon 5D.

Despite not living in the area anymore, Duff seemed to know everyone. He had no trouble convincing the desk guard to let them wander the premises unescorted. They walked around, stopping occasionally to shoot, speaking only in the hushed tones that the place demanded.

The more time Lovie spent with Duff, the more intrigued she was. He could go from jerk to gentleman in less than a second. And talk about hard to read.

She'd always considered herself a master at figuring people out. If she had to guess, she'd have said that whatever he was hiding had something to do with his family. He adored Ginny - who wouldn't? And he mentioned his mother often enough but completely clammed up when she asked about his father.

Sometimes, the best way to solve a mystery is to ask the right questions.

"So, has the B&B always been in your family?"

He paused, mid-focus, and turned to look at her, frowning. Her question was slightly out of the blue, but she thought the B&B was a good intro.

Duff resumed shooting along the fort's stone wall. "Gran and Granda opened it after the war. It was the only one in Inverness for a time."

"She invited me and Jo to move over there for the rest of our stay."

He chuckled. "Aye, well, she loves havin' the place full up, ye ken." He followed the flight of a bird with his lens before taking a few shots. "Business hasna been so good of late."

"Oh no!" Lovie turned to face him. "It's such a lovely little place. If it had been closer to town, we would have booked our stay there."

He nodded, smiling conspiratorially. "To tell the truth, I'm kinda glad things have been slow. Gran's not as spry as she used to be, though dinna tell 'er I said so. She'll box my ears."

Lovie laughed. "Was your mom anything like Ginny?"

"Ma? She was a wee fragile thing." His thumb stroked his full bottom lip. "Beautiful and kind," he added. "But fragile. Her strength was different than Gran's, ye ken. She was witty. Resourceful." She could see his love for his mother in his eyes.

Duff had impossibly beautiful eyes. The color wasn't unusual, not for a shallow sea in some warm climate. But the sea didn't stare back at you the way Duff was then. He searched her face, the wistful smile that had touched his lips fading.

"She was never the same after we left Inverness."

"After your dad?" *Left? Died?* She wanted to ask but hesitated.

He seemed to snap out of his daze. "Er...yeah." Emotions flickered across his face like home movies. He had some heavy stuff on his mind, but it was clear that he didn't like to talk about it. It was just as clear that he needed to. It hung in the air between them, whatever it was.

Duff leaned forward, resting his elbows against the railing, and stared at the rocks below.

"Did he..." Lovie edged closer. "Was there someone else?"

He glanced up, his eyes narrowing in thought. "Yeah, in a way." A sound from below drew his attention, and he lifted his camera to capture it. Lovie didn't care what it was. She was far more interested in what made this man tick. "The only person he ever cared about was himself. The rest of us were just baggage, ye ken."

"I'm sorry."

"Water under the bridge, and such." Duff squinted out over the horizon. Hardness edged into his voice. "It's just hard to come back here." She understood that perfectly.

"I know what you mean."

Lovie hadn't meant to speak her thoughts aloud. He turned those bright eyes to her.

"And your parents?"

"Mine are still together." She snapped a photo of nothing in particular. "On paper, they're the perfect couple."

"But it isna so in reality?"

"They seem content enough. I just always felt like something was missing between them. They married young, maybe too young, and grew apart, I think. But they stayed together."

"For you?"

She nodded. "Maybe. I like to think not."

"Why d'you say that?"

Lovie thought of all the forced smiles and false courtesy at their dinner table. She'd never seen any sign of affection between her mother and father. They loved her, of course, and raised her with a lot of joy. They just had none for each other.

"If I ever get married, I want it to be about more than duty and obligation. It's not that my parents don't love each other. I'm sure they do, in their own way. It's just that neither of them seems fulfilled."

Duff shrugged and unpacked his tripod, extending the legs. "It takes more than another person to fulfill you."

"I know that, but having someone you love who loves you. Someone who will be there for you no matter what, and not because they think they have to be. That's what I'd want."

"You're a romantic." Duff grinned over his shoulder.

Lovie smiled. "Maybe, a little. I do believe that sometimes there's a spark that happens between two people that you...you can't explain. It just happens. And then they're just...in sync." She shook her head. "I dunno."

"Aye, but you do. Don't you?" Duff focused that intense blue gaze on her. He stared for so long that Lovie began to shiver. He had a way of affecting her that she didn't understand. "Are ye cold?"

"No." She wrapped her arms around herself.

"Mmmph." He smiled, the sun glinting off his perfect teeth, and nodded over her head. "That's why I wanted to come today. Why I come here often when I'm home." Grateful for the change in subject, Lovie turned to take in the sunset.

Scotland was just one Kodak moment after another. In the distance, the sky was a riot of purples and blues, dipping into the pinks and golds that kissed the horizon. She was breathless, taking it all in, and cursing herself for having such a shitty camera.

She took a photo. "It's so beautiful."

"Aye. 'Tis."

Lovie turned back to find Duff staring at her with that knowing smile. His eyes sparkled in the fading sunlight. She forgot to breathe and then inhaled too quickly, dizzy from the lack of oxygen. Or him. Probably him.

Duff tilted his head regarding her. One chocolate wave fell over his eyes, making it look like he watched her from behind a veil.

"Yer one of those people that likes to poke at folk." His smile was playful, but his tone was staid. "Get 'em to tell you their stories."

Lovie squirmed under the scrutiny. He wasn't far off the mark. She did have a natural talent for it. She turned back to the water, snapping a photo of a passing boat in the distance. "You're interesting, is all."

"Interestin'?" She could hear the smile in his voice. The air warmed as he stepped closer to her side, raising his camera. "Define interestin'."

"If I could define it," she said, facing the lens. "It wouldn't be interesting, now would it?" He took a shot and then lowered his camera, one corner of his mouth lifting.

"She's interested in the interesting," he mused before taking another shot of her.

"Aren't you?"

He squinted at her question, edging even closer. "Aye, verra much."

A gust of wind blew a lock of hair into her face. Duff caught it. She held her breath as he coiled it around his finger before brushing it back out of her eyes. His thumb traced over her cheek, and she gave up breathing altogether.

Oh, God. He wanted to kiss her. She could see it in his face. Could feel the air shifting between them.

And she wanted him to kiss her. *Holy shit,* did she ever. He had that whole mysterioso thing down pat. Duff was gorgeous, talented, and funny. And freaking gorgeous. The kind of guy that wouldn't look at her twice back home. Jo, sure, but not her.

So, why was he leaning in?

And why wasn't she?

She tilted her head. Closed her eyes. And nearly jumped out of her skin when Bruno Mars blared from her pocket.

Duff blinked and shook his head, the smirk returning.

She laughed, pulling out her phone. "Hello?"

The sound of a speeding engine drowned out the voice on the other end. "Jo?"

"Hey, sweets! Where are you?" Jo sounded happier than Lovie had ever heard her. She frowned, shielding her mouth from the wind. Duff walked further down the platform, his shutter firing away.

"I'm at Fort George."

"You're at a fork?" A man's laugh broke through the background noise. Hamish, presumably.

"Fort, Jo. For-tuh." Lovie stuck her finger in her other ear. She could see Duff's shoulders shake with laughter. "Are you still with Hamish?" Duff glanced back.

"We're on our way to his estate," Jo emphasized the word 'estate.' Lovie rolled her eyes. He would have an estate.

"Don't tell me. He's a laird."

"Wouldn't *that* be something?" Jo was trying to temper her excitement, but Lovie recognized the giddy vibrato in her voice. If Hamish had an actual title, that would be the frosting on her TastyKake.

Did she plan to seduce this guy into making her his lady? Did that still happen in the twenty-first century?

"That...would be something."

"You have to come out here. It's gorgeous! Take a taxi. I'll pay." Hamish mumbled in the background. "Oh, that's perfect!" Jo juggled the phone, and Lovie heard the distinct sound of a kiss. "Ham says he'll get Duffy to bring you. It'll be a double date!" There was more mumbling from *Ham*.

"Oh, and bring a change of clothes. It'll be an all-nighter." Great.

Another phone rang. Lovie looked up to find Duff taking his out of his pocket, and she was suddenly in on both ends of his conversation.

"Hello?"

"*Hey ya, twally!*" Hamish yelled at him on the other end.

Duff met her eyes. "Eh!"

"*Fit ye on the day?*"

"Aye. Brought me camera up to the fort to catch the light. You?" Duff's Scots brogue thickened whenever he spoke to Hamish or his grandmother. Interesting.

"Ham's on the phone with him now," Jo said, unaware of Lovie's proximity to the man in question.

"Ah, you bodach!" Hamish laughed. Jo giggled. Lovie had no idea what the heck that was. She was pretty sure Jo didn't either.

She and Duff shared a look.

The scowl had returned. He wasn't too happy about his friend's interest in Jo. That was interesting and something she wanted to know more about.

"Come down to ma bit. Grab Joana's wee friend on that way. Will ye?" Duff met her eyes with a wink.

"Sure, awright. Do ye ken where she might be?"

He gave her a smirk that made something clench low in her belly. It should've been illegal to look at someone like that.

"Lovie, where are you? Duff is going to come get you." Hamish and Jo's tag team effort was irritatingly coordinated.

"I'm...uh...just getting back to the hotel." Duff looked at her with a shocked expression, his subsequent smile blinding her.

"Perfect! Grab a change of clothes, and we'll get Duff to pick you up. K?"

"I dunno, I—"

"C'mon, it'll be fun." In the background, Hamish echoed Jo's pleading. "You can even have your own room."

"Well, as long as I get a whole room to myself."

"Done!"

"Okay, then."

"Yay! She said yes." Lovie pictured Jo bouncing in her seat with excitement. She smiled despite her reservations.

"Joana says the lass is keen, so get yer arse over there and bring her here."

"Awright, see ye around about five."

"Barry!"

"Who's Barry?" she mouthed, raising her eyebrows at Duff, who just shook his head.

"He'll come get you around fiveish, okay? See ya, babe!"

"Bye." Lovie tapped her phone against her palm. "So, it's a...uh...a double date?"

A slow smile spread across Duff's lips. "Seems so."

AFTER A QUICK STOP at Gran's for an overnight bag and a not-so-quick stop at Lovie's hotel for her giant fucking suitcase, Duff drove out to Hamish's family estate. The land butted up against the shores of Loch Ness, and Duff knew that the girls would find it impressive.

Girls always did.

It had been in his family for over three centuries. Once five hundred acres, the land had been parceled out over the years, though the boundaries were invisible. The manor was grand enough to leave anyone with the impression that its owners were well-to-do. While the Mackays were comfortable enough, the estate was their biggest asset and technically belonged to a trust. Hamish lived in a smaller cottage at the loch's edge. If Lovie's friend had any caviar dreams, they would be quickly dashed. Though, that would probably be a good thing.

"If you're bringing me out here to kill me, just promise you'll make it quick."

"Wha?" Duff took a glance at Lovie. Only a quick one because taking his eyes off the path to the house was risky in daylight. In the pitch black, it was just plain stupid.

"I can't see anything past the headlights." She clutched the door, one hand braced against the ceiling.

He chuckled. "Dinna fash. We're almost there, and no one's going to kill ye."

It was hard not to watch her bounce with the car's jostling —very hard. She bounced very well and in all the right places.

Duff had wanted this girl since the moment he laid eyes on her. But she wasn't his type, the kind you love and leave. She was the kind you keep.

And to think he'd almost kissed her back at the fort. That would have been a huge fucking mistake. Epic. Duff didn't want to keep or be kept. He avoided attachments. Getting attached meant giving a fuck, and he had no more fucks left to give.

Not after having his entire family tried in the court of public opinion, not after being forced out of his boyhood home, and not after moving from town to town with his mother, doing whatever it took to survive.

Yeah, okay, he was a man. He had needs. And he'd never had a problem finding a beautiful woman willing to fill them, no matter where he was in the world.

Single serving fuckbuddies.

A little booze, a lot of charm, and they'd fall into his bed. But he never stuck around long enough to get to know them. Hell, sometimes he hadn't even bothered to learn their names.

Lovie let out a shriek.

Duff slammed on the breaks, throwing them both forward.

"Are you alright?" He checked her over, pushing her hair back. Her fucking Bambi eyes stared up at him, and his cock twitched. *Bloody hell.*

"I-I thought I saw something." Poor thing, she shook like a leaf. Duff peered over the hood and saw the cause of her distress.

"It's just a wee fox."

He inched forward after the creature dashed off into the night. "Are ye scairt? I thought you Americans were made of tougher stuff."

Duff took the road slower now, mindful of its inhabitants. Beside him, Lovie collected herself and made an indignant sound.

"We are, it's just...I'm a woman, and you're a stranger. And do they have electricity in this part of the world?"

"Aye, we're not complete barbarians. We jus' dinna see a reason to light the whole of Scotland."

"Why not?"

"Well, some animals only come out at night when they feel safe. If we lit every bloody mile, it would destroy the natural cycle, ye ken?"

"Yeah, I *ken*." She teased. Smart arse. "Very conscientious people, you Scots."

"Not all, but some." He pulled into the driveway. "Here we are."

"Was that an actual castle we just passed?" Lovie got out and walked to the back of the car.

Duff met her there to get their bags out of the boot. "That's the manor. Belongs to the family, but Hamish lives here in the cottage."

Her eyes went wide. "Cottage? This is bigger than the house I grew up in."

Duff laughed. "Aye, well, it's all about perspective, I suppose."

Lovie smiled up at him, and everything went still.

He was struck dumbfounded. Christ, she was so... Duff cleared his throat. "C'mon."

She followed him to the door, taking it all in.

It was a lovely place, he had to admit. Tranquil. Sometimes, it was hard to believe it was only a few miles from town.

Once inside, Joana whisked Lovie off to her room, presumably for some girl talk.

Hamish turned to him with a wolfish grin.

"This is shaping up to be a fine night, ma wee mannie!" He tousled Duff's hair, which he hated. Stepping away from the stairwell, he motioned for Hamish to follow.

"What on God's green earth are ye doin'? Bringin' her out here?"

"She'll have her own room." Hamish raised his hands, protesting his innocence, but his face had gone beet red.

"What of Sofia?"

"I'm no breakin' any vows, man. Calm down! It's just a—"

"*Wee bit o' fun*, yeah ye said as much." Duff shook his head. "I just...dinna understand why ye'd risk everything for it."

Hamish clapped Duff on the shoulder. "There's no risk. Now you, ya dog, what's up with you and that one?" He gestured toward the stairs where Lovie had just disappeared.

"Nothin'."

"Nothin' my arse, you two were gettin' pretty cozy out front. Don't think I didna see you."

Duff turned away, shrugging him off. "I don't know what you *think* you saw."

"Calm down. Christ, man." Hamish frowned. "Ye've been a right bastard since ye got home. Everything alright with ye?"

Duff straightened. "Aye, o'course."

"Is this about your da?" Duff spun back to him, and Hamish frowned. "Still?"

"No! It's not about him. I've nothing to do with him. Havna done for a long time!"

Rather than back off, Hamish stepped into him. "Awright, brother. Awright. Didna mean to touch a sore nerve." He put a hand on his shoulder. "You're not him, Duffy. You're a better man than he could ever be. You know that, don't you?"

Duff deflated from the pity in his voice. He met his friend's eyes. "Jus' leave it."

After a breath, Hamish nodded. "Done."

"Let's get this party started!" Joana bounded down the steps and headed straight to the whiskey cabinet.

"Where's Lovie?"

"Taking a shower. She'll be down in a few."

Hamish had a nice collection of eighteen and twenty-year-old whiskeys. Duff watched as she inspected the different bottles.

"I know nothing about Scotch."

"Well, I will have to teach you." Hamish joined the blonde at the bar.

Duff watched his best friend and Lovie's best friend come together in a fit of smiles and glances. He had become invisible.

"I'll, er, take my bag up."

This was so very, very wrong. He would have to say something before things got out of hand completely. He made for the stairs when something he heard stopped him cold.

"I can't believe a guy like you doesn't have a girlfriend."

The fuck?

Duff stepped back down into the parlor. Hamish peered over Joana's head and blanched like a kid caught with his father's girly magazines.

Oh, yeah. It was time to put a stop to this.

Hamish shook his head, pleading with his eyes. *Not now.*

"Soon," Duff mouthed to him before heading up the steps.

7

───────

OPENING DOORS

When he reached the first-floor landing, Duff closed the door behind him and cursed under his breath. Christ on the cross! He'd been back three days, and already he was in the middle of a mess.

He carded a hand through his hair and turned toward his room. A soft, musical voice halted him in his tracks. He'd warned Hamish about the latch on the bathroom door ages ago, and now it stood ajar.

The occupant, completely unaware of the exposure, continued her melody. The song was some annoying Christmas tune, but it sat sweetly on Lovie's voice. She passed by the small crack, and suddenly Duff couldn't breathe.

Her back was to him. Her skin a long pour of single malt that he wanted to savor.

Duff's eyes followed the slight curve of her hip as she dried off, obviously just out of the shower. He felt like a predator. Should've turned away and slipped into his room before she caught him peeping like a perv.

She was so goddamn gorgeous. He was so overwhelmed by the thought of tasting all of that fresh, dewy skin that his damned feet wouldn't move.

Lovie wrapped the towel around her body and panic gripped him. Duff hustled down the hall into his room, holding his breath as he stood behind his closed door. His heart beat wildly against his rib cage, the pulse pounding in his fingertips. His lips. His cock.

Only after he heard Lovie walk past, still whisper-singing the same tune, did he relax.

There was something about this woman that unnerved him. He'd told her things that he usually never spoke of aloud. Hamish would joke that maybe he'd finally met his match.

Duff snorted.

He'd never been down that road before and had no desire to make the trip. Besides, she lived three thousand miles away.

And then there was this thing with Hamish and Joanna. He needed to get him to come clean. Tonight. The lad was like a brother to him, but damn if he didn't drag him into some fucked up situations. He was supposed to stand up as his best man in little more than a week. If it weren't for him and his inability to find his arse with his own two hands, Duff might not be hiding in his room from a woman like Lovie.

"Ah, God," he chided himself. "Don't be stupid man. Ye'd be clot-heided to get involved with her."

A knock at the door sent him stumbling back. He recovered quick enough to answer and found - thank heaven for its sweet mercy - a fully-clothed Lovie on the other side.

"Hey." She smiled, warming him from the inside out.

Fucking hell.

"Uh, hey." Her sweater hugged her curves in the most distracting way.

"I thought I heard you in there. Are you coming down? Jo said something about food and I thought about trying my first Scotch."

"You mean to say you've never had whiskey?"

"I've had some, but not real Scotch." She shuffled from one foot to the other. Little tendrils of hair, damp from the shower, clung to her neck. He wanted to bury his face there.

Duff had to look away.

"Also, I don't want to be a third wheel."

Ah. Right. "Canna miss yer first taste of ambrosia, now can I?" Another blinding smile had Duff's jeans tightening. He wanted to strip her down and explore every inch of her.

This woman was definitely trouble.

THE LIVING ROOM, or parlor as Hamish called it, was pretty cozy for being such a large room. When Duff called the house a cottage, she thought perhaps he was being facetious. It was a cottage but on a grand scale. With ten-foot ceilings, a ginormous hearth with a mantel the size of a twin bed and enough comfy leather furniture to seat twenty, it was still a rather intimate space.

Too intimate for some.

Lovie had hoped that Duff would ease the discomfort she felt watching Jo moon all over Hamish. He may have looked like The Calum, but his personality left everything to be desired. Hamish was clearly more in love with himself than anyone else could ever be.

And yet, Jo hung on his every word. Even though every word seemed to be about him.

"I dinna want to brag, but-" Lovie hated the smug, self-congratulatory laugh that he did when he was about to do just that. Bragging seemed to be his occupation. Classic narcissist. "I went top o' the class that year. Duffy was what, third? Fourth?"

"Second." Duff sat on the back of a leather chair, staring into the hearty fire. Beside him, a nine-foot Christmas tree twinkled in red, green and gold. As picturesque as it all was, Lovie wasn't feeling particularly Christmas-y.

"Anythin' after first is hard to remember." Hamish laughed his stupid laugh, and Jo giggled like Julie Rabinow in the fifth grade. Trilly, and obnoxious.

"Second out of how many?" she asked Duff.

He turned to her, one dark eyebrow raised.

Lovie gave him a sympathetic smile.

He lifted one shoulder. "Outta a hundred and twenty, I reckon."

"Well, that's nothing to sneeze at."

"No, I suppose not."

Good God, he had no right to smile like that, so flirty.

Before she could say anything stupid, she looked away, only to find Jo grinning at her.

"What have you been up to these last two days, Looovie?" She winked, curling her tongue against her teeth like she was licking a secret. "You were fast asleep when I got in last night."

"Well, I walked through town. Took some photos." She glanced shyly at Duff. "Oh, and yesterday I went to a Christmas bazaar just off the river. They had some fantastic stuff there." Lovie omitted the part about her time with Duff and Ginny.

He met her eyes with a questioning grin.

"You mean the old folks fair at Eden Court?" Hamish huffed out a laugh. "They sell the same shite every year. It's for blue hairs and tourists."

"Well, I fall into one of those groups, so..." Lovie was tired of being around this dickwad. She glared at Jo who just shrugged and laughed at the smug joke from that smugging smugster from smugtown. *Mayor, surely. No, King.*

Lovie nodded at her own joke. "I need to get some air."

"You do that a lot." Hamish eyed her, lingering a little lower than was necessary.

"You got some sorta issue with yer lungs?"

"I just find it a little...stale in here." Lovie gave him her sweetest 'fuck you very much' smile.

"Eh Duffy, you should take her up to the roof." Hamish wiggled his eyebrows. "Lotsa air up there." Subtle.

"Yeah, sure." Duff seemed as thrilled with Hamish as she was, but he slid on his pea coat and motioned for her. "Coming?" Jo threw her another wink.

Lovie grabbed a tartan throw from the loveseat and followed him.

As they climbed the winding staircase at the end of the hall, Lovie tried hard not to stare at the firm ass of the man walking ahead of her.

Really, she did. They emerged onto the flat roof, facing the lake. It was another crisp, clear night.

Lovie smelled the fire from the chimney on the air and missed the warmth. She pulled the throw tighter around her and walked out to the railing. She could just make out the shapes of the trees and a few other homes across the way. So far away from the city, it should have been black as soot, but the full moon hung low on in the sky. It looked close enough to reach out and touch.

And the stars, oh... The stars were everything.

She tilted her head back and gazed up into space. It was Van Gogh's Starry Night in swirls of silver and the blackest blue. If she stared long enough, she might be able to see what Vincent saw.

Footsteps crunched behind her.

"Ye awright?" Duff shoved his hands into his pockets, hair fluttering in the breeze.

Lovie looked back out over the water. "Yep."

"I can go back in if yer wantin' to be alone."

"No, no. It's fine." She looked up and caught his half-smile.

He pulled out a bottle of Scotch.

"I didna come up empty handed."

"Where were you hiding that?" She laughed as he stepped up next to her.

"Deep men have deep pockets, ye ken." Duff passed her the bottle. The number on the front was eighteen. That was supposed to be a good thing, she thought. Large black letters above it spelled LAPHROAIG. She wasn't even going to try to pronounce that.

"I remember somethin' about you wantin' to try a proper whiskey."

"This looks pretty proper." Lovie sniffed the open bottle and promptly coughed. She would have recovered sooner if a strong hand hadn't begun thumping her on the back.

"I'm fine."

"Ye sure?" Now the hand rubbed in slow circles.

"Uh, yeah." Lovie leaned away, breaking the contact. She lifted the bottle to her lips, Duff's eyes following the movement.

"Slàinte."

Cool, liquid smoke filled her mouth. It was surprisingly smooth and not at all unpleasant. She looked at him, amazed.

He grinned. "Good?"

"Damn, I've been missing out."

His grin blossomed into a smile. Lovie handed him the bottle and he took a much more generous pull. Watching his lips purse over the mouth of the bottle, the same one she'd just drunk from, did funny things to her insides. Her brain went fuzzy when he swallowed, his Adam's apple bobbing.

He licked his lips. "This isn't the proper way to drink it, o'course, but I didna want to risk bringing any glasses up here."

"Good thinking."

Lovie accepted the bottle and took another, larger, sip. It tasted different now that his lips had touched it. Sexier, somehow. Both the liquid and the thought warmed her as they went down, giving her a nice, mellow feeling all over. That is until a stiff wind came off the water, pushing against her with icy fingers. She pulled the thin blanket up to her ears.

It made little difference.

Concern knit Duff's brow. "Cold?"

"I-I'm okay," she lied, teeth chattering.

He laughed. "You're not okay, lass. C'mere." Duff opened his coat and pulled Lovie inside, her shoulder resting against his chest. He wrapped one arm around her.

It was a startlingly intimate arrangement, and she inhaled his warm exhalations. He was a furnace, heating the side of her body that lay flush with his.

"Better?"

She nodded, her stomach in knots.

They fell silent and took turns drinking from the bottle. Being this close to him, it was impossible to deny her attraction. Every nerve ending was suddenly on high alert for the slightest twitch from the man beside her. He smelled of wood smoke and fabric softener, an intoxicating combination.

Lovie looked back out over the lake. The silvery edges of the waves glimmered in the moonlight, and she could just make out the silhouettes of animals foraging along the shore.

"Anything out here other than foxes?"

"Other wee beasties, but none to be afeared of." His near-whisper matched hers. "I lived here most of me life and never caught a glimpse of ol' Nessie." A chuckle vibrated from deep within in his chest.

"Oh, of course. I hadn't put the two together. Loch Ness, right?" She nodded toward the dark water.

"Yep. Spent a lot of time out there as a boy. We'd fish in the summer."

"You and Hamish?" He nodded. "It's hard to picture you guys hanging out together.

You two are so different."

"Are we?" He shrugged. "I s'pose we are, yeah. It was always him and me growin' up, though."

"You met at school?"

"Aye, at primary school. I was small for me age, always gettin' picked at by the older kids. One day, a few of the boys had me out in the field. They were wailin' on me somethin' fierce." Duff gestured with his free arm, animating the tale as most Scots did when telling a story. "Up comes Hamish, this big, braw lad with all that red hair, roarin' like a lion. 'If ye don't leave him be, I'll beat every one o' yer arses!'"

Lovie laughed, picturing it. "Oh my God, how old were you?"

Duff chuckled. "Eight and nine, I think, though Hamish was already taller than everyone else. Scared the shite outta those boys and me as well. We were fast friends after that. Me Ma practically adopted him."

Lovie smiled. "Tell me more about her."

He glanced down at her. "Me Ma?"

She nodded.

Duff took a slow breath and a slow pull of whiskey. "Why d'ya want to know."

"I just do."

He was quiet for a moment. Lovie thought he would ignore the query.

Duff tucked her head under his chin. It felt...right, somehow. "You remind me o' her, a little bit."

"Me?"

"Aye." He nodded against her crown. "Caring. Honest."

She flushed with heat from the compliment. "You have a high opinion of someone you've only known for two days."

"I'm a good judge o' character."

"I bet." Lovie tipped the bottle in his hand to her lips. "So, your mom?"

"Well, she was an artist, afore she met my father." He was silent for a moment. Lovie could almost hear the thoughts running through his head. "Not so much after. She had to work to help put food on the table. She was proud, ye ken. Wouldna take any help from me Gran and Granda."

"You're right."

"About what?"

"We are alike, at least in that way."

"Oh yah?" He smiled down at her. "Are ye stubborn as well?"

Lovie arched an eyebrow at him. "What do you think?"

Duff laughed, his shoulders shaking as he buried his face in her hair. "Aye, well, I wouldna call you fragile. Sensitive, maybe, but no fragile." He sobered. "Me Ma...she wasna built for this world. Not for him, anyway."

"Your dad?"

He ran his hand through his hair and nodded. "I dinna want to talk about it anymore."

"Okay."

"Sorry." He took a sip from the bottle.

"It's okay." The quiet of the night wrapped around them like a blanket. "It's sort of wild and magical here."

"Aye." His arm tightened around her shoulder and Lovie couldn't stop the sigh that escaped from her lips. The way Duff stiffened meant that he hadn't missed it.

She turned her face into his chest, and his hand slid under her hair to cradle her head, his fingers kneading the nape.

Duff took a deep, stuttering breath.

Lovie wasn't sure if it was her heart she heard pounding in her ears, or his.

Screwing her courage to the sticking place, she lifted her face to find him looking down at her, his lips slightly parted. Even in the low light, she could see the unmistakable desire in his eyes. He scanned her hair. Her face. Looked down at the non-existent space between them.

"This is a verra bad idea, love." He barely breathed the words.

"Yeah." She echoed his tone, shivering as his hand tightened, pulling her close. "The absolute worst."

Duff tilted his head and brushed his mouth over hers and then he claimed it.

Lovie was no blushing virgin, but nothing had prepared her for this kiss. It was, at once, delicate and luscious. Tentative, and demanding. Something she thought only existed on the silver screen, or in the pages of Jo's tattered paperbacks. He nibbled at her with lips and teeth. His tongue curled around hers, hot and sweet, and every synapse in her brain misfired.

Duff broke the kiss, set the bottle down and pulled her closer, tangling his fingers in her hair. Lovie tingled from her scalp down to her toes.

She slipped her hands underneath the coat and around his back, her fingers sliding over solid muscle and searing heat. They stared at one another, breathing heavily.

Lovie licked her lips before they came together again.

This kiss was decadent and full of promise. His mouth was soft, warm and urgent. He tasted like power restrained.

She gently bit down on his lip, running her tongue along the edge to soothe it, and Duff made one of the sexiest sounds she'd ever heard. She wanted to take him down to her room and see what other sorts of noises he could make.

His hand drifted down and over the front of her sweater.

Lovie's nipple peaked against the warmth of his palm, and a soft, needy sound escaped her throat. Her mind hovered in the shimmering haze between fear and desire.

Desire won.

She placed one hand over his, pressed it harder against her flesh and squeezed, knocked even more breathless by his answering groan.

Lovie came up for air, but there wasn't enough oxygen on the planet.

Duff leaned back, gave her a little 'wow,' and moved in for the kill, sucking on her bottom lip as if it were candied.

Lovie skimmed the stubble on his jaw with her fingertips and slipped a hand into his hair. His fingers tightened around a handful of hers.

Duff pressed her body to his, and she sighed into his mouth. She felt him, hard against her belly. They fit together like chocolate and peanut butter. Like Lois and Clark. Like Scotch and rooftop kisses.

His arm banded around her waist, nearly lifting her off her feet as the kiss deepened into something more than mere lust. It was magical.

A shout from the doorway broke the spell.

Duff leaned away, a shocked expression on his face. After a breath, he quickly set her down and removed his hands from her body. The cold air rushed back in with a vengeance. Duff took a step back, but his eyes were on her mouth.

Lovie could still feel his lips there. Indecision was written all over his face.

Yeah, me too.

"Duffy where are ye, ye bawheed? Pizza's ready." Hamish yelled from the top of the steps. His voice bounced off the eaves, grating against her ears.

Duff scrambled back. "I'm...sorry, I didna mean to..."

"No worries." Lovie cursed her breathy laugh. She pulled the blanket tight around her.

"Heat of the moment."

"Right." Duff frowned, but his eyes drank her in. "Yeah. Look, we should-"

"Right."

She followed him back down the steps, torn between thanking Hamish for saving her from herself or killing Hamish for, well, cockblocking.

8

———

DISCOVERIES

Lovie hated the smell of nail polish, but they'd somehow ended up in her room after dinner. It was the same back home. Jo blew on the nails of her right hand. She'd painted them candy apple red, the same color as Hamish's convertible, apparently. It matched the red in the paisley quilt on the bed.

"I think Duff's into you."

Lovie looked away, the blood rising in her cheeks. She flipped through a worn, leather-bound book containing the history of the estate. Judging by the portraits of his ancestors, Hamish was the product of some powerful genes. His family had a long history. At another time, he might actually have been a laird or something. "Nah, he's just being nice, keeping me company while you work your magic on the Calum."

"Nice? The way he looks at you, he's being more than nice." Jo's freshly painted toes nudged her thigh. "Did something happen between the two of you?"

"What?" A sharp edge slid along Lovie's finger as she flipped the page. "Ouch! No!

"Why would you-? W-What about you and the Calum?"

"It's Hamish," Jo said his name as if it were a title. "And no. Not yet."

"Are you playing coy?"

"Believe it or not, no." She shrugged. "*He* is."

Lovie laughed. "You're kidding."

"I know, right?" Jo gaped. "He flirts like crazy, but he backs off whenever I hint about taking it to the next level."

"Well, huh."

Jo went over to an ornate, maybe even gilded, full-length mirror. It was one of two in the small room. "Maybe he's not attracted to me."

Not attracted? Jo had to be suffering from some latent body dysmorphic disorder. She turned this way and that, assessing her near-perfect figure.

Lovie sucked in her stomach.

"Do you think he might be gay?"

"I don't know," she replied. "I doubt it. He seems way too interested in your tits."

Jo turned to her, grinning. "Really? Not that there'd be anything wrong if he were gay, but it would explain a lot." She checked out her ass in the mirror. "Oh! Maybe he and Duff are-"

"No, Duff's straight." It came out more forcefully than Lovie meant it to. " Or he could be bi."

Jo glanced back at her, puzzled. "Maybe. You said he hasn't made a move."

Oh, he'd made a move. Or she had. Either way, Lovie didn't trust herself not to blurt it out. She slammed the book shut and went over to the bookshelf that sat by the window.

It was old. Everything there was.

"It didn't come up in conversation, Jo."

"Doesn't matter. I only have a few days. If I can't get Hamish to make a play, this whole trip will have been a bust."

"We could always go down to Glasgow early. Find another Calum for you there."

"What? After all of the effort I've put into this one? Hell no. I will crack this nut tonight. Literally." She bit her lip, grinning.

"Um, ewww."

"Hey, I was going to say 'suck him off,' but you're such a lady." Jo curtsied.

Lovie laughed. "You're disgusting sometimes."

"It's why you love me." With one last flounce of her hair, Jo went to the door. "Wish me luck!"

Worried, Lovie grabbed her hand. "Just be careful, 'kay?"

"That's my middle name." Jo winked. The door closed softly behind her.

Lovie flopped onto the bed and stared at the ceiling. She needed to see Duff. Whether it was wrong or not, what happened between them earlier was amazing. Her lips still tingled from that kiss. She hoped they would get another moment alone to explore whatever was brewing between them. Not that she would ever see him again after the week was through, but they'd formed a kind of friendship. She hoped, at least, to stay in touch with him.

Oh, who was she kidding? She wanted that boy, and bad.

Lovie checked her hair in the less-ornate mirror. After trying to run a brush through it, she gave up. If ever there was a lost cause.

Duff's room was only two doors down from hers, but her palms were sweaty by the time she'd walked the fifteen feet of carpeted hallway. She took a breath, rubbed them on her thighs, and knocked.

Booty calls were so not her thing.

He opened the door, wearing nothing but his jeans. They were unbuttoned, and, just like that, so was Lovie's brain.

Holy mother of pearl. His chest was a wall of muscle. His stomach a rippling, slalom course of masculine goodness. An inky trail of hair led down from his navel and disappeared below his open waistband. When she lifted her eyes to his, one eyebrow was arched over his piercing blue gaze.

Duff had the kind of eyes that smiled even when he wasn't.

He let out a heavy sigh. "Lovie. Whadya want? Come to ask me more questions?"

"What? No, I...uh...I-" His reaction to her appearance at his door was markedly cold for someone who had his tongue down her throat a couple of hours ago. Had she imagined the intensity of their moment on the roof? Her mind went blank. What was the proper protocol for a botched booty call? She stood there, hoping for rescue. *Throw a girl a bone...er.*

He sucked his teeth and backed away, swinging the door wider for her to enter. It was the only welcome he offered. Lovie stepped gingerly into the room.

Duff's space was larger than hers, furnished more like a lived-in room than a guest room. The bed was a king to her queen. An armoire filled one wall, and there was only one mirror, which sat atop a dresser. Lovie walked over and ran her fingers over the armoire's intricate carvings.

"This is gorgeous."

The door closed with a thump. She looked back to find Duff leaning against it, his legs crossed at the ankles.

"It's an antique. Probably original to the house." He shoved his hands into his pockets. Beside him, on a small table, sat the bottle of Scotch from the roof. It was much closer to being empty.

Lovie was taken aback. "Are you drunk?"

"No' nearly enough." Duff rubbed his eyes. He seemed so tired.

"Did something happen?"

His head popped up, eyes wide. "How can you ask me that?"

Suddenly, Duff was on his feet and moving toward her. It wasn't that she was afraid of him. She wasn't. It was the intensity of the look on his face that backed her up into the armoire.

"What happened on the roof should never have happened."

Oh. Duff's words would have been a cold splash of water on her simmering desire if the hunger in his face weren't quite so apparent. He still wanted her.

He dropped his eyes, and Lovie had to catch her breath. Her lungs burned as if she'd been underwater too long.

"Why not? Am I that bad a kisser?" She tried to cover with humor, putting her hand on her hip to hide the shaking.

"Because you and I have got nothin' in common, and I know your type. You canna just be about the sex." His voice, deeper than before, rumbled from his chest like thunder.

Lovie straightened. "Are you saying that because I'm a woman?" Duff lifted his chin in response. "You don't think women just want to get laid sometimes?"

"O'course they do, but not you, hen." His eyes swept her from head to toe, something that — five minutes ago — would have dropped her panties to the floor. Now, it just pissed her off.

"What makes me so different?"

"Ye just are!"

"Like you know me!"

"You sure as bloody hell don't know me, do ye?" He glared at her.

What had changed since the roof besides the conspicuous consumption of the twenty-year-old whiskey?

"Asking all yer questions like we're on a bloody quiz show. Diggin' up me past." He barked out a laugh. "Is that your idea of seduction, because I'd havta say yer sorely lacking."

"You're drunk."

"So what if I am? What's it to you, *Luuvie*?"

Lovie seethed. "You're an asshole."

Duff smiled, and that stopped her short.

Okay... Maybe he'd been hoping to get a rise out of her, but to what end? She cocked her head, studying him.

"Or at least you want me to think you are."

He frowned and stepped back. Something like fear flickered behind his eyes. "Come again?"

She knew she was on to something. "You're hiding."

He laughed out loud then and crossed his arms, his biceps bulging. "From what, pray tell?"

"I dunno, but you shroud yourself in sarcasm to hide your...your...cherophobic tendencies."

"My what? D'you call me a cherub?"

"No, a *cherophobe!* It's someone who's afraid to be happy. Someone who willingly sits under a thousand-ton emotional tower, waiting for it to collapse. Almost hoping for it!"

Duff's eyes narrowed, his lip curling. "Don't tell me. You took a Psychology course at university."

Actually, she had minored in it, butLovie huffed with indignation. She would have made a great therapist, dammit. "That's not the point."

"It's entirely the point!" Duff brushed by her, reaching for the scotch. "You think you have some rare insight into my psyche. Let me hand you a clue, darlin', ye don't." He took a swig, slamming the bottle back down. "Ye don't know me, and, trust me, ye don't want to."

"Because you're, what, dangerous? A loner? Some kinda bad wolf?" Lovie crossed her arms. She was growing bored of his pity party. "You're just a lost soul determined to stay lost."

"Jesus, d'ye ever listen to yerself?" Duff turned away from her and stalked toward the window. "Since ye want to know all about me family history, I'll give ye the short version." He faced her, bracing his arms inside the window frame. They were really, *really* nice arms. And his six-pack had come with two freebies. Wow.

Stay focused, woman.

"You want to know all about *Ma,* and *Da,* and me fucked up child-hood, and all the reasons why I stay the fuck away from Inverness, aye?"

Lovie gave him a short nod, uncertain if she really did want to know now that he seemed inclined to tell her. *Too late to back out now.*

"My father was a grifter. Ye ken what that is? He conned people out of their pensions, tricked old ladies into givin' up their savings for some petty scheme o' his." He exhaled, some of his fire fading. "For years, Ma had no idea the money that put food on the table, put clothes on our backs, had taken the food and clothing from someone else. She never knew. None of us did. Me Da never worked an honest day in his miserable life." Duff's long arms dropped to his side, his fingers clenching and unclenching.

"It was a clever little racket he had--him and two others. And when they were caught, it was all over the national news. Our family - me Ma, me Gran, and Granda - were...the talk o' the Highlands. I was in sixth form at school." He glanced at her. "Like your senior year in high school." She nodded, thinking back to his comments about moving around a lot. He sagged into the wide window seat.

Despite her desire to go to him, Lovie stayed glued to the spot.

"Ma refused to pull me out of school mid-year, so I had to see me classmates every day." He picked at a spot of peeling paint on the frame. "The teasing didna bother me so much. Hamish had me back an' all. It was more the look from some of the parents and teachers who knew his...his victims. Some of them were their family, ye ken. Ma lost her job. People shunned us. And Granda...his heart..."

He swallowed hard, breathing like he couldn't take enough oxygen into his lungs.

Lovie didn't want to hear any more. She didn't want him to relive it for her.

"We buried him that summer before Ma and I left for Glasgow." Lovie gasped.

He looked up, a stricken expression on his face.

Tears stung the back of her eyes. *God!* She was always doing this, needling people. Always trying to dig deeper and get them to show what they wanted to hide. Duff was so right about her. She did think of herself as some sorta amateur analyst, but she'd been arrogant. And way, way out of her depth. And yet, she still wanted to help him, somehow.

When he spoke again, his voice was quiet. The pain and regret almost palpable. "Ye'd think I woulda learned from me father's mistakes, but no." He let out a bitter laugh. "I was a right bastard to her. Me ma did everythin' she could to put me straight. Didna want me to get liftit, ye ken. Arrested. Every time I fucked up, we had to move. I didna care, tho'. I was angry. I blamed her." He closed his eyes and took a hiccupping breath. "In the end, it's my fault she's dead."

She stepped toward him. "Duff, no."

"Aye," he said, defeated. "It is."

Lovie didn't know what to do or how to help, but the distance between them was unbearable. Watching him tear himself apart hurt.

"I wore 'er out, you see. I couldna see past me own pain. Couldn't see what it all had done to her, losin' her home, her husband, and her father. I was such a shit."

He fell silent, lost in his memories.

Lovie wanted to ask what happened to his dad but kept a quiet distance. The least she could do was let him wrestle with the demons she had dredged up. Despite the warm air, she shivered with shame. What had she done? He'd been so helpful. Kind, even. Sweet.

She had no clue how to help. Maybe it was best to leave him alone. She turned toward the door. Before she could reach it, she was blocked by a six-foot-three, Duff-shaped barrier.

Lovie nearly lost her footing, stumbling back from him.

His eyes were dark and focused squarely on hers. Searching. Angry. Maybe even desperate. She should have been afraid. After all, she didn't know the guy. But Lovie was drawn to him, pulled in by his intensity. His pain. His need.

His eyelids fluttered shut, the lashes smudges of thick soot against the red of his cheeks. His restless fingers had pulled his mop of espresso-brown locks into clumps. Lovie wanted to smooth them back. Soothe him.

Duff muttered something under his breath as if arguing with himself, then dragged her into his arms. He wiped some wetness from her cheeks.

She hadn't even realized that she'd been crying.

Lovie grabbed onto his shoulders just before he lowered his face to hers. He licked the salt from her lips, a move so unexpected she gasped.

His arms closed around her, holding her fast against his hard body while he whispered fevered words of longing against her neck.

How he didn't want to want her.

How he was close to losing his mind.

His tongue traced the shell of her ear, and Lovie's knees threatened to buckle. It was so intimate. So carnal. His large hands circled her arms tightly, possessive. Duff slid his hands down to hers.

"Duff, I'm sor—."

"Don't." He shook his head slowly, the waves of his hair brushing her cheek like fingers. "I shouldna done that."

"I wanted you to," Lovie confessed. Despite his rage and his pain, she ached for him. Perhaps more so now.

Duff raised his head to look at her. He frowned, touching his forehead to hers. "Why?"

"What?"

"Why would you...with me, why?" There were still demons between them.

She slid her fingers between his. "Duff, those things that you told me about your dad. You think you're like him?"

"Apples and trees." He dropped her hands and shoved his back inside his pockets.

"He wasna with us in Glasgow, or London, or New York, but it didn't stop me from..." He shrugged, deflating. "I'm not a good man, Lovie. I've done things. Got his blood in my veins, ye ken."

"Our genes don't determine everything about us, Duff. You were just a heartbroken kid, acting out. But you're not that kid anymore. Right?" She waited until he met her eyes. "We choose who we want to be." Lovie touched his cheek because she couldn't stop herself. There was a war raging behind his eyes.

"I've tried my whole life to be different, but I'm just the same. I do the same stupid, selfish-" He stopped abruptly. "Look, I dinna know why I keep pouring this shit out to you. Sorry." He squeezed her shoulders, his hands warm and strong.

"It's okay." Lovie tried to keep the pity out of her voice. That was the last thing he needed to hear, but her heart was breaking for him.

He released her.

"You should go." He was locking her out already. Shutting down.

Lovie took his face between her hands, and Duff met her eyes, a question in his. She knew the answer. "No, I shouldn't."

9

―――――

REVELATIONS

At first, it was too fast.

Duff's voice, rough with emotion, ghosted over her skin as he caressed her face, her neck. Murmurs of *'make me crazy'* and *'want you so much'* made Lovie's nipples tighten almost to the point of pain.

He kissed her as they stumbled toward the bed. The kiss evolved into a clash of lips and teeth and tongues. The hands on her ass were a little too rough. Her fingers in his hair pulled a little too hard.

Then, it wasn't fast enough.

Duff broke away from her mouth and released her. Lovie took a step back, struggling to catch her breath.

His hand cupped her cheek.

She placed hers over his heart.

Duff studied her face. Searched her eyes. Lovie didn't know what he was looking for. Didn't know what he needed. There was pain in his gaze but also passion. Hunger.

He ran his thumb over her bottom lip, and she stepped into him, flattening her hands against his chest.

Lovie felt like they were swimming against a strong current, neither wanting to rush things but needing to do just that. She went up on tiptoe.

Duff touched his forehead to hers and pulled her flush with his body. He was hard and ready against her belly. *Damn.* Lovie bit her lip.

"God...your mouth." The way his voice had dropped yet another octave had her shaking. He teased her, nipping at her lips and chin. Skimmed over her neck and then gently bit down.

Lovie lit up like a Christmas tree. Her clit throbbed as she rubbed up against him, desperate. Her panties clung to her skin, soaking wet. The air filled with gasps and urgent moans, most of them hers.

She wanted...needed...something.

Anything.

Everything.

Now.

Before she could find the words, Duff's hands slid up her back, under her tee and lifted it over her head.

His hand fell to her zipper, and then her jeans fell into a pool at her ankles. Duff wrapped his arms around her - God, so warm and strong and solid - and then she was airborne as he picked her up and laid her on the bed.

He leaned in and attacked her mouth like a man possessed. Duff demanded everything with his kiss. Left her nowhere to hide. It was terrifying. Exhilarating.

This was what they'd all been writing about, she thought, *those romance writers—this aching need to connect or die trying.*

Lovie ceased thinking at all when he captured one of her lace-covered nipples in his mouth, crying out from the unexpected pleasure. She ran her fingers through his hair. His hands never stopped moving, deftly stripping her bare. Even as his teeth grazed her breast, he kept stroking her skin, marking her with fire.

He moved back and looked down the length of her body. "Sweet, heav'nly lord."

Lovie trembled under his gaze.

Duff met her eyes and smiled. "Yer so..."

He reached up a shaky fingertip. Ran it across her lips and down her chin, her neck. Down the valley between her breasts. Down and down. The finger parted her flesh and curled inside her. Lovie gasped, her back arching.

"Jus' beautiful."

Lovie couldn't wait anymore. She sat up and grabbed at his waistband. Taking the hint, Duff stood up to remove his jeans, his gaze always on hers.

He stood naked and still, breathing heavily, at the edge of the bed.

She let her eyes do what her fingers couldn't, frozen as she was at the sight of him in the flesh. His body looked as if Bernini had hewn it from marble himself. Powerful but lean, and not an ounce of fat to be found. Self-conscious, her hands went to her doughy thighs.

"Don't do that."

"What?" God, she sounded so turned on, which she was, like, whoa.

"Don't hide."

"I wasn't."

"You were." His voice was low and throaty. So unbelievably sexy. "You don't need to hide."

"Easy for you to say when you look like a lost Gosling brother." She tried to smile, but his eyes devoured her.

Duff crawled onto the bed like a panther, forcing her to lie back. His cock brushed against her thigh, and she glanced down. Her whole body clenched with the need to be filled by him.

"You did that to me." He nuzzled his nose against her cheek. It was the only point of contact as he hovered over her, the muscles in his arms barely registering the strain. "You do this to me."

He flexed his hips and hissed as Lovie rubbed her leg along his length.

"Duff..."

Balancing on one arm, he grabbed his wallet from the side table. Lovie ran her hands down his chest and stomach, marveling at the ripple of muscle beneath his skin. He sat back on his haunches and ripped open the tiny, square packet in his hand. Lovie collapsed onto her back, liquid with anticipation. He covered himself, groaning, and then he was over her again. The bed shook as he slowly lowered his mouth to hers.

"Now, Duff. Now." She tried to pull him closer. It was like moving a wall.

"Easy, love, or this could get embarrassing for me."

She didn't care.

Lovie grabbed his ass with both hands and pulled him into her body. The groan was mutual.

Finally, he was inside her. A sense of relief washed over her, so strong that she let out a sob. He felt so good. Had it ever felt so good?

Duff lifted his head, looking down on her with concern.

"Did I hurt ye?"

"No...no." She smiled up at him, lifting her knees and inviting him deeper.

He groaned and nudged her thighs wider.

Her muscles fluttered around him.

"Christ." He locked eyes with her again, his usual Caribbean blue looking more like Atlantic gray.

"Please, Duff."

He moved, and she dissolved, wrapping her legs around him as she tried to absorb him completely. Be absorbed by him. Duff murmured against her neck, words she couldn't make out but understood.

"Oh God..." Flames of pleasure licked between her thighs.

He silenced her mouth with an urgent tongue as his pace increased, pulling her right to the edge of bliss.

Lovie scraped her nails down his back, swallowing his guttural moan. He broke the kiss, panting.

"Fuck, Lovie...ye feel so good." His eyes were unfocused. His lips swollen. She could feel him barely holding onto his control, and her body flushed with female satisfaction. She took his face between her hands as he lowered his forehead to hers, his eyes closed with concentration.

"Don't hold back." She swiveled her hips.

"Wait! Fuck, wait I...I want you to..."

She met his eyes and rocked under him again. "Don't hide."

With a groan, Duff withdrew. He grabbed Lovie's hips, flipped her over, and pulled her upright to her knees. She whimpered at the loss of him.

"What're you...?"

"Shhh, I've got ye." Duff knelt behind her, his legs on either side and slid his arms around, holding her flush to his chest. Large hands cupped her breasts as he pressed his open mouth against her neck. His teeth nipped at her skin. Lovie melted against him, her hair cascading over his shoulder.

Lovie felt him trapped between them, hot and hard. Why was he holding back?

The hand on her right breast slid down. Down her stomach and between her thighs, his fingers combed through the damp curls and found her clit.

"Fuck...you're so wet." His breath was hot against her cheek.

She arched against him. "You did this to me."

"Fucking incredible." His other hand tweaked her hypersensitive nipple.

Lovie whimpered as tiny explosions sparked behind her eyes. She grabbed his thighs for leverage and rolled her hips against his hot, thick fingers.

"Yeah, that's it." Duff's mouth moved to her ear. "Come for me." Lovie shattered.

The orgasm crashed through her with a ferocity she'd never experienced, stealing her breath and her reason. Tendrils of ecstasy curled throughout her limbs as she shook.

He held her close, his breathing as ragged as hers, still hard as steel against the small of her back.

Lovie's body felt light and empty, and her mind floated in an airy bliss. She melted onto her stomach.

Duff ran his tongue along the globes of her ass, up her spine. "God, that was beautiful."

That was one word for it. "Wow," was all she could manage.

He tilted her hips and parted her sensitive, quivering flesh, entering her with a soft grunt. Her aftershocks reverberated around him, and he shuddered with each one. As good as it was, it was no good. Lovie needed to see him. She straightened up and turned around, pushing him onto his back. It was her turn to drive.

AT THE FIRST touch of her tongue, Duff's mind fractured. His head lolled against the pillow, and his fingers dug into the sheets as she moved up his body.

Lovie licked a line up his stomach, his chest, along the cords of his neck. Even the dimple in his chin. She ran her lips and hands and tongue over his collarbone, his earlobes, the corners of his mouth. She was barely touching him, and he was dangerously close to exploding, holding onto his control by a thread.

"Please."

"Now *you're* begging?" Her husky laugh almost sent him over the edge. Then she straddled his hips and sheathed him in her slippery heat, and he nearly blacked out.

"Jesus."

Brushing his shaking fingers over her face, he pulled her forward. She licked her full lower lip, making his brain trip another circuit. He nipped her parted lips.

"Kiss me. Please."

Fuck. She was so needy and so open. He kissed her. Drove up into her until they were rocking together, faster and faster, the headboard drumming against the wall like a bodhran.

Lovie sat upright, panting. "Show me what you want."

Duff's hands curled around her waist, and he stilled her, held her aloft. Withdrew. Waited until she met his eyes.

Raising his hips, he teased her entrance. Lovie gasped, suckling him with her body as her sex clenched. The slight swell of her belly clenched and relaxed. Her breasts, full and round and creamy, rose and fell with her breaths. The look on her face was pure rapture.

He was mesmerized. Determined.

Up. Circle. Down.

Up. Circle. Down.

Duff used his strength to control his thrusts, building a steady rhythm.

Lovie's muscles fluttered around him. "Duff...oh...yes..."

She threw her head back, and her hair brushed the backs of his hands. So soft. *Fuck!*

She was so soft, inside and out. He couldn't believe she'd let him in. Him.

Lovie leaned forward, her palms on his chest.

Their eyes locked.

She was glowing. Radiant.

"Yer beautiful."

She smiled, her hair a red sun setting around her. "So are you."

There was so much more than desire in her eyes. It shot through him like electricity. A little moan escaped her throat, and his balls tightened. There were jolts of pleasure everywhere they touched.

He surged up into her, dangerously close, but he needed her to come one more time. Needed to feel it.

Duff sat up. Cradling her head, he rolled them over and kissed her long and deep. He gently bit down on her nipple, and she clenched around him.

He built up a rhythm and buried himself inside her. She was so wet, so warm, so perfect.

It was heaven.

She was heaven.

Lovie arched against the bed.

Nudging her legs further apart, Duff stroked deeper, and she made a sound somewhere between pain and pleasure. She was hot and smooth and tighter than a fist.

She let out a long, low moan and grabbed the headboard. Duff pressed her knees up toward her shoulders and stroked through her cock-strangling climax. He'd been so busy watching her pleasure play out on her face that he was blindsided by his own.

It bowed his back and ripped her name from his throat, spiraling through him like an errant firework. His body splintered into a thousand pieces.

Duff collapsed into Lovie's arms and held her close. He turned his face into the crook of her neck and just...inhaled. Shampoo and whiskey and Lovie.

He listened to her breathing settle and felt her stomach move against his. Soft hands stroked his back. Soft lips kissed his shoulder.

Duff tried to hold onto some small portion of his sanity—no such luck. Three days in, and he was stupidly into her. He'd known it would be this way. Fuckin' knew it.

After a while, he rolled over and sat up. The cooler air of the room raised the gooseflesh on his skin. Grabbing a few tissues, he quickly cleaned himself up and tossed the refuse into the wastebasket.

He flopped onto his back, turning his head to look at her.

Lovie lay beside him, limp and languid. He spied a tear running down her temple and sat on one elbow.

"Lovie?"

"I'm okay." She smiled up at him, and he flooded with relief. Sprawled out naked on the bed, the moonlight filtering in through the window to paint her honeyed skin with silver, she was a vision.

"That was..." She took a shaky breath and gave him a smile that reduced his spine to loose pebbles.

"Aye." Duff cupped her cheek and leaned in to kiss her. Lovie smiled against his mouth, teasing him with little nibbles. He lifted his head to look at her, and she met his eyes. He wondered what she saw. They barely knew one another, but it didn't feel that way to him. No, it didn't.

Not at all.

They kissed again, moaning softly into one another. He only stopped because his head was spinning.

She pushed him onto his back, threw one leg over his thigh, and rested her head on his chest. His fingers slid into her hair. The urgent need to consume her temporarily abated, he had time to luxuriate in the soft, fragrant coils.

Duff had never felt this kind of harmony.

Lovie was incredible. Sensual, playful, and shy, and nothing like he'd ever experienced. She was also fearless.

His head hadn't been in the right place.

She should have run screaming from the room. Instead, she'd given herself to him in such a way that he had no choice but to give right back. It scared the shit out of

him.

He'd just made love to her. Not shagged, not fucked, made love.

It may have been a first.

Lovie turned away, putting her back to his front, and he spooned her. Generally speaking, he wasn't the spooning type. Generally speaking, he didn't do this. Intimacy.

The women he had been with over the years, they'd meant nothing. He'd felt nothing outside of immediate gratification.

Lovie sighed, and there was a twinge in the vicinity of his heart. Hope stirred in the place where his soul had lain dormant.

It felt foreign and right and good.

Too good.

He wrapped himself around her. Nuzzled into her hair. Took her scent into his lungs.

This was something.

She turned her head toward him. "Do you have anything to drink besides Scotch?" "Ah, no." Duff sat up and peered over her shoulder.

She had a dreamy, satisfied expression that made him want to roar with

pride. "I can get us some water, or-"

"Water would be perfect." She smiled, her eyes already closing.

He kissed her shoulder. "Be right back, then."

Duff slid off the bed and stepped back into his jeans. The duvet had been pushed to the floor.

Lovie lay curled on her side, her arms wrapped around her. He couldn't get over how trusting she was. How completely she'd chipped away at his defenses.

A clock chimed somewhere in the house. It was almost Christmas Eve. Would Lovie want to spend it with him and Gran? Joana could come too if she wanted.

Maybe he had time to get Lovie something small. To show her that he'd been thinking of her.

Duff smiled to himself, shaking his head. *You're in trouble, me lad.* He gently covered her and slipped out of the room. He'd made it halfway down the hall when he heard a familiar rhythm.

Bang. Bang. Bang. Bang.

The closer he got to the primary bedroom, the louder it got.

Bang-bang. Bang. Bang.

"Oh God! Don't stop!" *Mother.*

Fuck.

Duff was going to kill him.

10

DEPARTURES

Lovie woke up, acutely aware of the lack of a warm body next to her. The light filtering in through the windows told her that it was well into the morning. Had Duff come back to bed last night?

She needed some water. She also needed to pee. Her muscles protested from abuse as she got out of bed, but it was a welcome ache. Making love to Duff, and that's what it was, had been a revelation. But what now? She didn't even know where he lived.

She dressed quickly because the room was freaking cold. Apparently central heat hadn't reached the Highlands. Out in the hall, she listened for the sound of the other occupants, but it was church-quiet. Where was Duff?

After using the bathroom and brushing her teeth - no morning kiss with funky breath, thank you - she crept downstairs.

Duff sat scowling in front of the fireplace, poking at the crumbling logs.

"Hey."

His head snapped up, his brow knit with a frown before a soft smile curved his lips. "Hey."

"You...didn't come back."

"Shit." He ran a hand over his face and came over to her. "I'm sorry. Your water.

Hang on." He started toward the kitchen, but Lovie stopped him, wrapping her arms around his waist. He hugged her close, his body deliciously warm against her chilled skin.

She looked up. "I can get it."

"I lost track o' time." He smiled down at her, but there was sadness in his eyes.

Lovie frowned. "Everything okay?" Duff nodded, smoothing her hair back from her face. He was so powerful and yet so gentle.

"Yeah, I just...needed to think."

Oh no. *No, no, no.* She knew that look. Was he really going to hit it and quit it?

"You're not, I mean..." She couldn't stop staring at the non-existent spot on his chest. "You don't regret-"

"Oh, God no!" He squeezed her to him so hard it was difficult to breathe, but who needed air?

"No." He kissed her softly, cradling her face in his hands. "No."

Lovie smiled with relief. "Good. Me neither."

"Good." His was only a half-smile.

Something was up, but she'd done enough pushing in the last twenty-four hours. After everything they'd shared, he'd tell her in his own time. He patted her bottom as she turned for the kitchen.

Jo wasn't in her room when Lovie made it back upstairs, and her bed hadn't been touched. Apparently, she'd sealed the deal with Hamish. And good for her! Rumpled sheets all-around.

Lovie grinned, the highlight reel of her evening with Duff running through her head. He seemed a little distant just now, but she felt assured that it was nothing to do with what happened between them.

Relatively assured.

He was probably still thinking about his father and all the things he'd told her. They'd talk some more about that, when he wanted to. *If* he wanted to.

It wasn't until after she'd showered and dressed that Jo made an appearance. If there had been any doubt that she and Hamish had danced the horizontal mambo, the goofy expression on her face eliminated it.

"Good?" Lovie grinned.

"Ohhhh yeah." Jo high-fived her as they tag-teamed the bathroom. "We'll have a tell-all sesh when we get back to the hotel."

"Cool."

Should she tell Jo about her own evening? It almost seemed too special to share, but she was dying to tell someone.

Citing some family obligation, Hamish asked Duff to drive the girls back to town. He and Jo shared a long kiss goodbye, but Lovie was more interested in the death glare that

Duff threw their way. It was positively murderous.

Just what the hell was that about?

DUFF WAS SO close to going ballistic, he barely kept it together. Of all the selfish, reckless, pig-headed things Hamish had done in the years he'd known him, this was the worst. The absolute fucking worst.

The drive back to town had been torture. Joanna sat in the back of his car, smiling from ear to ear while Lovie - sweet, beautiful Lovie – looked over at him like he hung the moon.

He was a fucking liar.

When they arrived at the hotel, Joanna kissed him on the cheek before she bounced away, leaving him and Lovie alone.

"Are you sure you're okay?"

"M'fine." He hugged her to him, resting his chin on the top of her head. She was so thoughtful, and he didn't deserve it.

She gripped the sides of his coat like she'd never let go. He hoped to God she wouldn't, when she learned the truth.

"I need to take care of somethin', and then I'll call ye. Awright?"

Lovie leaned back and smiled up at him. "Awright." He had to laugh.

"I'll turn ye into a Scot yet."

Her eyes went wide, and he stopped breathing.

What had he just said?

Jesus, Joseph, and Mary...

He kissed her quickly and let her go, before he said some other bawheeded thing.

Lovie waved from the door as he left to find - and throttle - the alleged groom.

Duff stopped home to check on his gran, who wanted him to stay for lunch. He knew that she sensed something was wrong, but begged-off sticking around. He needed to straighten this mess out if he could.

He caught up with Hamish at MacKinnon's, where he was already three pints in with Roger.

"There he is!" Hamish slurred, grinning like an idiot.

"What the fuck do you think yer doing?"

The redhead's eyes popped. "I'm havin' a pint with my wee mannie here, and wondering what bee's gotten into yer knickers."

"I heard you."

"Come again?"

"Last night."

Hamish had the good sense to turn beet red, but then shrugged. "Yeah?" He grinned over his pint glass. "Well, I hope you took lessons because I gave it her good."

"You fucking asshole."

"Calm yer tits, man!" Hamish laughed, grabbing his arm. Duff shrugged him off.

"Ye've got a bride, or had you forgotten?"

"Couldn't damn well forget with you remindin' me every other minute, now could I?" Hamish set his glass down hard on the table.

"What's goin' on, lads?" Poor Roger looked back and forth between the two of them.

"And what about Joanna?" Duff clenched his fists, astonished by Hamish's lack of remorse. Did he even know the man anymore?

"None o' yer concern, really though." Hamish stood slowly. "Is it?"

"Aye." Duff stepped into him. "'Tis"

Roger leapt to his feet. "Now, boys. Let's no' go an' do somethin' ye'll regret."

"You get some cocoa on yer cock, mannie? Is that it?" Hamish sneered. "And now you think ye've got to defend her friend's honor or somethin'?"

Duff introduced his fist to the redhead's jaw with a satisfying crunch.

"I'M HUNGRY." After Jo finally stopped recounting every detail of her night with Hamish, both of them had fallen asleep. It was late afternoon before Lovie awakened from some very vivid dreams. Or memories, really. Dreameries?

The way Jo kept going on about Hamish's stamina and prowess, Lovie got the impression that it wasn't all that. She also felt less and less inclined to share her own experience. What she and Duff had shared...it had rocked her world. She fought hard to curb the urge to call him, but damn if she didn't really want to hear his voice. See him.

Feel him.

Wow, Lovie, get a grip.

"So. Foodage. Want to go down the pub?"

"Down the pub?" Jo giggled. "Listen to you, picking up the lingo. Yeah, let's go. The guys can catch up to us later." She stopped, grinning. "And listen to me! The guys. We have guys, Lovie! Well, I mean..." She turned to Lovie, unsure. "You and Duff..."

"What about me and Duff?"

"Anything you want to share?" She smirked.

"Nnn-nope." Lovie smiled sweetly. "Let's go eat."

The sun was setting by the time they got to MacKinnon's.

Lovie was beginning to think of it as "their" pub, hers and Duff's, but also Jo's and

Hamish's. A few days ago, she felt like an outsider but, after meeting the boys and Ginny, she was beginning to like Inverness. A lot. Maybe they could skip Glasgow and stay there another week.

They opened the door to the pub and stepped into the middle of a scene straight out of Fight Club. A wall of bodies stood between them and the action, but it was clear by the shouting and cheering that someone was about to get a beat down.

Lovie was ready to make a joke about Scots and their tempers when she heard a familiar voice.

"…and tell her that you're fuckin' gettin' married!"

Lovie looked down at Jo, who apparently had caught that too.

"Was that Duff?"

She tried to peer over the group of men, but it was no use. They were caught up in an ale-infused, bloodthirsty frenzy, chanting for one of them to pummel the other. All she caught was a shock of coppery, red hair. Hamish.

"What the fuck is your problem? So what if I took the girl tae bed? What's it to ye? Just because I'm gettin' marrit, doesna mean that I'm dead." There was laughter in the crowd. "Besides, you got yours, ya ned. And dinna say you didn't. I know that moony look on yer face."

"Shut up." Duff's voice was clipped and cold. "Shut yer gingin mouth, you twally fuck."

Lovie didn't need to speak like a local to get the gist of what was said.

From the look on Jo's face, neither did she.

The crowd surged as someone threw a punch. They whooped and cheered, and the noise was deafening.

Lovie felt sick to her stomach. She stumbled back.

Hamish? Engaged? Couldn't be. Poor Jo! Duff wouldn't lie about something like that, would he? Then again, she didn't know him at all. Not really. Had it only been three days since they met? And she'd already fallen into bed with him. And poor Jo!

Shit!

She tried to take a breath. It smelled of stale beer and greasy food.

There wasn't enough air.

It was too loud.

Too many people.

Too much commotion.

Too much.

"Lovie?"

The sickening sound of crunching bone sent her reeling. Lovie spun around, feeling for the door while bodies buffered her on either side. Over the din, she heard the grunts and groans of the two men.

Jo grabbed her arm. "Lovie, come on. Let's get out of here."

There was a great roar from behind them, and they both turned around. Lovie found herself staring right into Duff's eyes as he stood over Hamish, who was on his knees, his face contorted with pain. He had the redhead's arm twisted at an odd angle. Duff had a bruise blossoming on his left cheek. A spot of blood spread from the corner of his mouth.

"Lovie." She saw her name on his lips. Then Jo pulled her out the door.

The cool air rushed in around her as she stumbled after Jo, down to the river's edge.

Jo grabbed her arms and pushed her down onto a bench. "Sit."

"What just...what were they..."

"Don't worry about it, Lovie. Just breathe, okay? You're scaring me."

Lovie looked up, confused, and saw the terror in Jo's eyes. "I'm okay."

"You were practically hyperventilating in there, babe."

"Oh...Jo...I'm so sorry, Hamish-"

"Forget Hamish."

What? "What? But I thought-"

"Yeah, about that. I may have exaggerated just a bit." Jo displayed about two inches between her thumb and index finger, and Lovie sob-laughed with relief. "Look, fuck him. I'm more worried about you! I've never seen you this upset. What happened? Is it Duff?"

"Lovie!"

She turned to see Duff running toward them.

Jo sprang to her feet and intercepted.

"What the fuck did you do?" She grabbed his collar and jerked him around to face her.

Lovie had never seen her so angry. He tried to talk over her head.

"I'm sorry, Lovie. I-" Jo slapped him. The crack of it startled a few birds from the trees.

Duff froze, squinting out of one eye while his hand shielded the other.

Lovie found her feet and her voice. She stood and looked him in the eye.

"So you and your mate both got fucked, huh? Had a good laugh?"

"God, no! It wasna like-"

"Is Hamish engaged?"

"Lovie, please."

"She asked you a question. Is. Hamish. Engaged?" Jo's voice was icy.

Duff jerked away from her with a groan. "Lovie."

Jo moved between them again. "It's a yes or no question, Duff."

"Yes." He met Jo's eyes, his own eyes clearing. "Sorry, Joanna. Yes, I'm...I'm so sorry, I..." He looked up at her.

There was a mixture of fear and anger in his face. Lovie could give two shits about his fear or his anger. Or the purple bruises forming on his eye and cheek.

"He's engaged, and you said nothing, to me or to my best friend." Her voice sounded foreign to her ears.

"Yes."

Lovie closed her eyes and took a shuddering breath. When she opened them, both Duff and Jo were staring at her. "Thank you for the truth."

Lovie turned on her heel and walked briskly toward the hotel.

Dodging an irate Jo, Duff ran to catch her. He grabbed her arm and jumped in front of her. She turned to stone.

"You really don't want to be touching me right now." She couldn't even look at him. The hand on her arm made her stomach roil.

Duff let her go as if he'd been burned. "Lovie. Just...let me explain."

"Please move." Her body shook with fury. Her mind was boiling in it. It gnawed on her gut and threatened to explode from her kneecaps in the general vicinity of his groin if he didn't move. *Right the fuck now.*

"You won't even hear what I have to say?" Lovie turned to him. Duff's face went blank, his eyes stony. "O'course not. Why would you?" He took a deep breath and moved aside.

She walked away. Didn't bother looking back.

Jo caught up to her a few minutes later. She'd heard their voices fading into the distance. Jo had given it to him good.

She'd never been prouder.

When they reached the hotel, she walked past Jo and into their room. The door closed, and it took everything she had not to start screaming and breaking furniture.

"Are you okay?"

Lovie looked back at Jo, incredulous. "Am I okay? Me? I'm pissed as hell. Are you okay? How dare he string you along like this? Who does he think he is?"

"Lovie-"

"Assholes, both of them! We need to leave here. Right now."

"Lovie!" She stopped mid-tirade. "What happened with Duff?"

"Why are you asking me about Duff? Hamish is the one whose eyes you should want to claw out. And why aren't you more upset about this?"

"Because I kinda already knew."

It was then that Lovie noticed Jo's red-rimmed eyes. She'd been crying.

"I'm going to kill him." Lovie started for the door.

"No!" Jo jumped after her. "It's not worth it. I'm okay. Really, I am."

"Then why are you crying?"

Jo sagged onto the bed. "Because I'm a fucking idiot. Who does this stuff but me? Flying to Scotland to find a book boyfriend. What's wrong with me, Lovie?" Jo dissolved into tears.

Lovie scooted next to her and pulled her into her arms. "There's nothing wrong with you, babe. You're just a hopeless romantic."

"I'm pathetic." She sniffled.

"Well...yeah, but you have a big heart and a lot of love to give."

Lovie handed Jo the tissues from the nightstand. "What I don't understand is why you're not angry with Hamish. I'm mad as hell."

"About Hamish? Or about Duff?" Jo blew her nose. "I'm assuming he didn't tell you."

"No. He didn't." The tears that Lovie had been fighting threatened to spill.

"Lovie...did you and he, I mean..."

Yeah. They had, but she couldn't even think about it. He'd been lying to her. A lie of omission was still a lie. Maybe he hadn't been so wrong about himself after all.

Even thinking that sickened her, but she was so angry. She couldn't stay near him another minute. "I know we're supposed to stay another day, but I need to leave this place. Like, now."

"Tonight? On Christmas Eve-eve?"

"Yes, if we can. Or tomorrow morning?"

Jo took one look at her and nodded. "Okay, chica. Whatever you want. I'll get on the phone."

Lovie needed distance. Home wasn't a possibility for another week, unless she wanted to pay through the nose. Duff had already cost her too much.

Glasgow would have to do.

11

ARRIVALS

Lovie welcomed the anonymity of a big city. Glasgow had been a welcome retreat from everything that happened in Inverness. Jo moved their reservation so that they didn't have to spend one more night in Duffville than necessary.

On Christmas Eve, they sat in George Square listening to a children's choir and stuffing themselves with cream cakes. Christmas Day they exchanged gifts and watched Netflix in their hotel room. It was nice. They'd spent the week since taking in the sights, though Lovie had floated through them in a daze.

Jo had secured an invitation to a New Year's Eve party, but Lovie wasn't in the mood. The truth was that she felt like she'd left a part of herself behind. The question was, would she ever get it back?

"You okay?" Jo curled her eyelashes in the mirror.

"Yeah. I'm fine."

Ever since Inverness, their roles had been reversed. Jo had taken up the mantle of the mother hen, making sure she ate and slept and showered. Lovie didn't know what was wrong with her. She felt like she'd been turned inside out.

Maybe it was the flu.

Jo sat on the bed. Her sparkly, silver dress riding up on her thighs. Lovie wondered where the rest of it was.

"Look, my mom always says run as fast you can toward your dreams. And if a guy can catch up to you, marry him." She stepped into a pair of impossibly high heels. "No one's caught me yet, but I'm still running." One corner of her mouth lifted as she squeezed Lovie's hand.

"In those heels?" They shared a smile. "I'm sorry about the trip."

"I'm not!" Jo exclaimed. "As for Hamish-" She shrugged. "Sure, he looked like The Calum, but he was a total douchebag. I knew that even before...you know. And he sucked in the sack, so good luck to whats-her-name." She grinned and then turned serious.

"Honestly, I've had a great time, all things considered. For one, I've never seen you lose control. It was worth it for that alone."

"Whatevs." Lovie grinned, shaking her head. "Thanks for...I dunno. For being you." Lovie squeezed her hands, grateful.

"You wouldn't want me any other way." Jo gave her a nudge. "So...nothing else from Duff?"

He'd sent her a text on Christmas. No more apologies, just 'I hope it's merry.'

"No." Lovie released Jo's hands and stood. "And I don't expect to hear from him anymore. I think I've made it pretty clear that I want nothing to do with him."

"Are you sure that's what you want?"

Lovie's mouth dropped open. "After everything, you can still ask me that?"

"Of course! He made you happy." Jo seemed completely unaffected by his betrayal. "Sure, he fucked up, but he wants to make amends. That makes him a good guy in my book. And you know how I am about my books."

Lovie wrapped her arms around herself, forcing away the memory of his. "He's the worst kind of guy. He pretends to be one thing but, really, he's another."

"It wasn't Duff's idea for Hamish to lie to me about Sofia. He lied to Duff too."

"Sofia? So, that's her name. Anyway, whether it was his idea or not, he didn't tell me. Or you."

"He did, though. Plus, I think he broke Big Red's nose on my behalf."

"Only because he got caught out!" This conversation was damaging Lovie's calm. All week she'd tried to push Duff out of her thoughts.

It had been easier during the days. Unlike Inverness, Jo had never left her side. Not even when she met a bona fide Gideon in the VIP room at SugarCube.

Jo dragged her to museums, shops, and restaurants, never letting her stop long enough to brood. They'd ridden the hop-on-hop-off tour bus, taking in every sight on the route.

The days were cake, but the nights...the nights had been friggin' awful.

Duff invaded her dreams, whispering words of desire in her ear until she woke up feverish and aching for his touch. Or crying, hating him.

"Look, I don't want to talk about Duff, it just pisses me off more."

"Because he matters to you."

"I only spent a few days with the guy, it's not like we...like we were..."

"Falling in love?"

Lovie let out a bark of laughter.

Love?

Seriously?

The guy was a mess. And the *son* of a mess. Feeding her some sob story about his family, probably just to get into her pants. And she didn't even know his full name! Or where he lived, for that matter.

He was probably lying about being a photographer. Except that she had seen his work, and it was incredible.

But so what?

Stupid jerk. With his opalescent eyes and cupid's bow mouth. And that body.

Okay, sure. He fucked like a god, and could be so unbelievably sweet, but he was also a lying liar who lied.

Love.

Hmmph.

"You need to step away from your Kindle, Jo."

"I understand why you're upset, believe me I do, but you're wrong, Lovie." The humor wicked away from Jo's voice so quickly that Lovie's head snapped up. "I talked to him."

"You what? When?"

"He came by the hotel the morning that we left Inverness. Not to see you, but to see me."

"What for?"

"To apologize. The way he talks about you..." Jo had that dreamy look in her eye. She was such a hopeless romantic, even after Hamish. "All I've ever wanted was someone to talk about me that way."

Lovie shrugged. "Talk is cheap."

Jo studied her for a moment. "What would it take?'"

"For what?"

"For you to let him back in." She offered a sad smile and pulled on one of Lovie's curly locks. "I've never seen it before, you letting someone in. Other than me, of course."

"It doesn't matter. I didn't matter enough for him to tell us the truth." Lovie closed her eyes against the onslaught of emotions. "There's no coming back from that."

HE MUST BE crazy - stark raving mad - to think it would make a difference, but he was all out of options.

Joanna knew Lovie better than anyone. If she thought he still had a chance, he had to take it. He'd been shocked as hell to get her call and broke land speed records to get there in time. *Be honest with her.* She'd said. *She needs to know that she matters to you. It's simple.*

Simple.

Nothing about this was simple, but Duff cracked his neck, walked up to the door and knocked. A shadow passed in front of the light the other side. The figure moved toward the peephole, and then there was a gasp.

"Lovie?" He took a step forward, catching her unmistakable 'stay the hell away from me' vibe through the door. "I know you're there, love." Silence.

He double-checked the text that Joanna had sent to his phone after she left. It was the right hotel. Right floor. Right room.

Hopefully, it was the right thing to do.

Duff placed his ear against the door. He could hear her breathing. "Won't you let me in so we can talk? Please?" He ran his fingertips down the surface, tracing the lines in the grain of the wood, wishing it were her skin. "I've come all this way."

The bell from the lift sounded. Two girls emerged, each dressed to the nines and carrying bottles of champagne. They flashed bright smiles, and he nodded. One of them winked as they passed him. "Happy New Year." He nodded.

Behind the door, there was silence. Time for plan B.

"Awright. Jus'...I'll leave this for you. Okay?"

Duff unzipped his jacket, his fingers shaking, and pulled out a large envelope. After kissing it for luck, he slid it under the door, held his breath and listened for any movement. Watched for any change in the light.

The shadow moved toward the door, and hope flared in his chest like a well-struck match. One excruciatingly long minute passed and Duff couldn't take it anymore. He knocked twice.

A second later, the door opened and his heart stopped.

She'd obviously been crying. Her eyes were puffy, and her cheeks were drawn. The knowledge that he was the reason sliced into his gut like a dull knife.

Her hair was an untamed mess of curls, spiraling out in all directions.

She wore a white tank top and the most hideous pajama bottoms he'd ever laid eyes on – SpongeBob yellow with bright pink dots that made his head hurt. He wanted to kill them. With fire.

She looked ridiculous and adorable and sad. And she was the most beautiful thing he'd ever seen. He wanted to scoop her up and kiss her pain away.

"You've got two minutes, and then you've got to go."

Okay, so she wasn't in the mood to forgive and forget.

"Before I turn back into a pumpkin?"

She crossed her arms, closing herself off even further, but moved to let him inside.

Not the time for jokes, you idiot.

"How did you find me? Jo?"

He nodded. And thank God she'd called him. He'd been ready to leave Inverness for his next assignment, in Kabul. Who knew when he'd be back on the grid?

"I wanted...clarification."

She frowned. "On?"

"Where we stand."

"I thought I made it pretty clear."

Duff followed her further into the room, with its standard chain hotel decor. Beige carpet. Colorful, abstract prints on the walls. As good a place as any to get your hopes incinerated.

Lovie moved behind the desk, putting it between them. His envelope lay there, unopened. She crossed her arms again and stuck out her chin, but tears shimmered in her eyes.

God, he couldn't stand to see her like that. A steel band tightened around his heart. "Lovie-"

"What did you think this would accomplish?" She gestured to the envelope on the

desk.

"Well, you havna read it, so not so much."

"You wasted your time coming here, Duff." She swallowed hard. "Go home."

"No."

In three days, Lovie had broken down every single one of his defenses and zeroed in on his fears and insecurities. She'd awakened a part of him that he thought he'd lost forever. Duff hadn't come this far for her not to know how much she meant to him.

How much he missed her.

Needed her.

"No?" A flicker of panic showed in her chocolate brown eyes. "What do you mean no?"

He softened his tone, but it was now or never. "I mean not until you read it. Read it aloud to me."

Lovie looked at him as if he'd sprouted a second head, but Duff stood his ground. Sh huffed out a disbelieving laugh. "Fine."

After a brief stare-off, she snatched up the envelope, hesitating a moment before she tore the end open. Her hands shook, and Duff wanted nothing more than to take her into his arms.

Lovie gasped when she saw the photo.

He couldn't believe that it had only been eight days since they shared that first sunset at Fort George. He'd stared at the picture for hours, memorizing every twist of her hair. Every freckle on her cheek. The way the colors exploded behind her, framing her like the work of art she was.

She cleared her throat, flipped it over, and began to read.

"To the One Who Matters." Her eyes flickered up to his, and she took a breath before continuing. *"To the One Who Matters, I am sorry. I should have told you everything in the beginning. Chalk it up to misguided loyalty to someone I thought was my friend. And stupidity. Mostly that last thing."*

A smile tugged at her lips, and she covered it with the back of her hand.

"I should have told you before we...especially after, but I didn't. And I can't blame it on my father or anyone else. I was just so scared - terrified - of losing you when I'd only just found you. You deserve better, and I can do better. Be better."

The first tear fell, and Duff took a step toward her. Just one, because she held up a shaky hand.

"You are infinitely braver than I'll ever be, and I'm a coward. I'm a

coward because, now that I've seen what life is with you in it, I don't want one without you. And that scares the hell out of me."

"God...Duff..." She frowned, shaking her head.

"Keep reading," he whispered, desperate for her to understand. He inched closer, every cell in his body screaming for him to touch her. Show her.

Lovie swallowed hard. When she resumed, her voice trembled. *"I have felt every single mile that you've put between us. The distance has been slowly carving into me, and I can't bear it."*

A sob broke from her throat.

"Go on. Finish it."

She shook her head, the tears falling freely now. "I...I can't...I-" She dropped the photo on the desk.

"It's okay. I know what it says." Duff moved in front of her. He was so close now that he could smell her shampoo. "It says...that...you unlocked a part of me that I never knew existed. And when you left, you took it with you." He tucked a lock of hair behind her ear. "So, I'm here to claim what's mine."

"Duff-"

"You knew I would follow you, didn't you." He gently took her face into his hands, smoothed away her tears. "You wanted me to follow."

She met his eyes, and Duff tried to show her everything. Everything that he was. Everything that she was to him. Everything that they could be if she wanted it.

He drew her against him and kissed her deeply. She felt like home and tasted like salted caramel. A little whimper escaped her throat before her hands came up between them and she leaned away, breathing heavily. They both were.

"You knew?"

"I...hoped." He offered her a small smile, she looked so desperately torn. It broke his heart. "I had a little help, though."

Lovie pinched the bridge of her nose. "Dammit, Jo."

"It wasn't Jo, it was you."

"Me?" She was cute when she was so clueless. "I didn't even know myself."

"Let me see, what did ye say?" Duff squinted as if trying to remember. In truth, her words were carved onto his ribcage. He captured her eyes in his, so deep and soulful. "There's a spark that happens between two people that you can't explain. It just is. And then they're in sync." He smiled. "Sound about right?"

Her mouth had dropped open and she snapped it shut, the corner lifting slightly.

"That's rude, you know."

He stifled a laugh at her expression. "What is?"

"Using my words against me."

Duff pulled her close again. God, it felt so damn good to hold her. When she didn't move away, that flame of hope in his chest became a bonfire. "Let me stay, Lovie. For New Year's."

She pulled her bottom lip between her teeth, chewing on what he knew what the softest thing he would ever taste.

"I'll get a room here. Or at another hotel nearby," he added quickly. "Let me stay."

"How can we, after everything? And the distance-" She dropped her eyes away but her hands curled into his jacket, pulling him in.

"I have a feelin'..." He placed a soft kiss on her cheek. "When ye wake up tomorrow, you'll realize that this is the beginning of somethin' amazing, and I'd like to be here when that happens." Her eyes closed.

"Damn." She took a deep breath, fighting the smile on her lips. "That was perfect."

Duff felt the knot at the back of his throat loosen. "I rehearsed."

His fingers discovered an exposed patch of skin at the small of her back. She was even softer than he'd remembered. How was that possible?

"You're crazy." She shook her head.

"About you, yeah." Optimistic, he dipped his knees to meet her eyes. "Can I stay?"

She laced her fingers behind his neck, and Duff's heart started beating again. She smiled at him, and he just stared. Amazed. Relieved.

Her smile faltered. "No more lies."

"Never again." He held her gaze. "Never. Can I stay?"

The shy smile returned to her lips. "At least until morning, but it would be better if you stayed here. Don't you think?" Lovie placed a gentle kiss on his grateful mouth. "I have to see if this prediction of yours comes true."

Duff touched his lips to her forehead. "God, I missed you." He ran a hand up into her hair. Tilted her head and claimed her mouth with a slow, leisurely kiss.

Lovie wrapped her arms around his waist and buried her face in his chest.

Duff held her tight, her curves molding to him. Perfect. He hoped to God he didn't fuck this up. He smoothed a hand over her hair. Ran his fingers up and down her back, over her shoulder. Over and over.

She sighed and pressed herself against him. "What's your name?"

"Huh?" Duff was busy discovering each one of the constellations on her skin. She had freckles on her freckles.

"Ginny called you C.J."

"Oh, it's Calum."

Lovie leaned back, her eyes wide. "What?"

He traced the outline of her lips with his fingertip. "Calum James MacDuff."

THE END (for now)

CALUM ME MAYBE

CALUM ME MAYBE
XIO AXELROD

1

THIRST TRAP

Calum MacDuff was hungry. Chew-his-own-arm-off-hungry. And thanks to the teeny, tiny nightshirt barely covering the woman on the screen of his tablet, he was fucking starving too.

Said Vixen bent to open a cupboard, giving him a view of her soft, round ass, and he groaned aloud.

"I hate you."

"No, you don't." The words were delivered with a saucy shimmy.

Duff laughed. "You're a cruel, cruel woman, Lovie Grant."

"Moi?" A bright smile lit up the screen as she straightened and turned toward the camera, red curls framing her heart-shaped face. "I just needed another pan for the bacon."

"Ugh, you're killing me here."

"Don't they have bacon in the desert?" She teased as slim fingers plucked the crispy strips from the pan. It was the thin, fatty American kind, but bacon was bacon.

"Sure, at the hotel back in Marrakesh, but that's at least a ten-hour drive from where we are." Duff's eyes followed the path of the bacon from Lovie's plate to her mouth, unsure of which he wanted to taste more.

"And yet you have Internet." The corner of her mouth tilted up into a half smile as she drew the tip of her thumb into her mouth and hummed with pleasure. "Bacon good."

Bloody hell. "I can go without many things, but I canna do without seeing your pretty face as often as humanly possible."

"Sweet talker." Lovie's blushing grin pixelated, and Duff slid his palm-sized WiFi hub closer to the makeshift window of his bivouac. Now he could watch her move in HD. And he was damn glad he was alone for the moment.

Duff shared the portable shelter with his usual partner-in-crime, video journalist, Archie Lee. There was also a medic named Steven and his assistant, Malek, with whom Duff and Archie traveled during the day. Malek drove their hulking Defender through the desert sand with skill and more than a little recklessness.

The organizers of the Marathon Des Sables, a grueling trek across a particularly barren stretch of the Sahara Desert, had thought of nearly everything. Satellite calling stations were set up daily so participants could remain in touch with friends, family, and sponsors. Trekkers were allotted one free email per day on the race's official Internet service.

That just wouldn't cut it for Duff. He always traveled with a satellite device.

All of their gear had been dumped shortly after setting up the tent. Bed rolls, backpacks, and other equipment sat in tiny piles where each man had claimed his space. Steven took the largest, as contestants frequently visited him throughout the night. Thick canvas groundsheets covered the bottom surface area, allowing at least a psychological division between them and the sand beneath. He knew he'd find bits lodged in every crack and crevice, every pair of his boxer briefs, for months to come.

A bin bag slumped in the corner, filled with the day's refuse. Each member of the race party, participant, staff, or observer was responsible for helping to keep the desert clean for the locals. Duff admired the initiative but couldn't imagine living in such unrelenting heat.

Only a month ago, he would have paid anything for it. Photographing polar bears in the Arctic Circle, he had thought his fingers would fall off. Taking on so many extreme assignments was taking its toll, but the money was good. And it was an adrenaline rush. Still, Duff shuddered and pulled out fresh keffiyeh, stripping the sweat-soaked cotton scarf from his head. He almost wished he were back on that unforgiving ice road to Nunavut. The sun would set soon, dropping the thermometer from one hundred-seventeen to forty-two Fahrenheit. Duff would welcome the respite, as short-lived as it might be.

On screen, Lovie frowned. Her lips pursed with worry. "You look so miserable. Maybe you should have taken a job closer to civilization."

"Aye, I'm miserable. I'm tired and hungry and horny. But no other gig would pay even half of what they're giving me for this one."

"I wish I could help you." She cooed while leaning against the counter, giving him a nice view down her top.

"You could help me with one thing." Duff wiggled his eyebrows. At least, he thought he had. He'd lost the ability to feel his face after an unexpected dust storm had descended upon them. He didn't have a mirror but was sure it now resembled a piece of tanned leather.

"Ohhhh no. No, no, no. I am not getting you off online." She used air quotes around the hardly dirty words. Adorable. "Someone could be hacking or phishing or whatever you call it, and then my luscious boobies would end up on Instagram."

Duff dropped his eyes south, remembering how luscious they'd felt in his hands. In his mouth.

He groaned, smiling. "No doubt making the world a much better place." He caught a flash of white before his view was blocked by something. "Lovie?"

The obstacle was removed, replaced by her gorgeous, heart-shaped face. "Yes?"

"Did you...did you throw a towel at me?" He chuckled.

She moved off-screen, and Duff heard a drawer open, followed by the sound of cutlery. When she returned, she held a full plate of bacon and eggs in one hand and a fork in the other. Lovie slid her laptop back, affording him a better view, and settled herself at the counter.

"Are ye going to eat that in front of me?"

"Does it bother you?" She lifted a forkful of eggs to her mouth. A string of cheese trailed from the plate to her plump lips. Evil, she was.

"And if it did?"

"You could always log off." She slid the fork into her mouth and closed her eyes. At that moment, Duff found being away from her unbearable. She was his...lover? Mate? Erstwhile girlfriend?

He hadn't a clue what she was. What they were. All he knew was that he'd logged more hours online in the past eight months than he had in the past five years, and had loved every second of it until now. He wanted her. And that bacon.

Duff's stomach growled, settling at least one argument. "And what's that you're drinking?"

"Something I made up," she said smiling. "A spiced apple spritz. This one is virgin, but I think it would be nice with a bit of your favorite whisky."

"You are a wicked tease. I'm in the middle of nowhere, with nothing but cereal bars and dried meat, and there you are, enjoying that lovely meal and talking about sharing a dram." Lovie paused mid-chew. He watched the tiny crease form between her eyebrows. The one that said she was more worried than she let on. "Hey, I'm only kidding. I'm okay."

She set the fork aside and leaned forward. "Are you sure?" One delicate hand moved toward the screen. Duff closed his eyes and imagined those fingers tracing his features. In their short time together, it seemed to be one of Lovie's favorite things to do.

Duff often wondered if she did it to memorize him, the same reason he'd taken hundreds of photos of her. To keep her close.

"So..."

"Yeah?" He opened his eyes to find her face filling his screen. Her eyes stared directly into the camera. As always, it took his breath away. And scared him shitless.

"Any idea when you'll be on this side of the Atlantic again? Miami seems like eons ago." She'd flown down to meet him when he was on assignment in the Keys, and it had been one of the best weekends of Duff's life.

"Soon."

"Yeah, I've heard that before." She shook her head, piled high with the ringlets of her fiery, red hair. "I honestly don't know how you do it. You've been on one assignment after another since Edinburgh."

"I know, and I'm sorry about that."

"Don't apologize for doing your job. I know how much it means to you." Lovie smiled, but Duff could see the uncertainty on her face. "I just...wondered when we'd actually occupy the same space again." She sat back, her gaze dropping back to the screen.

"I have to swing through New York soon. Philly's not that far, right?"

Her eyes lit up, and it ignited a firestorm in his gut. "About ninety minutes, by train or car."

"There you go. I'll come for a day or two. Might even be able to squeeze in a week."

She flashed a brain-melting smile. "A week? You sure you could handle me for that long?"

Nodding, he exhaled quickly as he flipped through his mental calendar. Duff couldn't bring himself to tell her it was more likely he'd only have forty-eight hours to spare. "Easy peasy. So, I'll see you soon?"

She nodded, her acceptance tentative. Understandably. He'd made similar promises before and broken them. They were to meet in London, but then he'd been offered a chance to shoot in Dubai. Miami was supposed to be four days, but he cut it down to two when he accepted a last-minute gig in the Outback.

Lovie hadn't complained, not verbally, but Duff could read the disappointment between the lines of their frequent texts and emails.

Truthfully, he didn't know why he hadn't visited her more often or had her come to meet him. The concept of a long-distance relationship was still new. Hell, the whole *idea* of a relationship was new. He was afraid he'd screw it up before it had a chance to start—if they had a chance at all. They'd already weathered one storm of his creation.

But with Lovie, he had all of the benefits of a serious relationship with none of the nasty side effects. Namely boredom. Or petty misunderstandings that blew up into arguments. On paper, the situation itself was perfect for him.

She got the best of him, which was easy in small doses. He got the very best of her. Duff figured that the less time he spent with Lovie, the less likely he was to drive her away. And how was that for fucked up reasoning?

He was surprised by how much he missed her, and not just physically. Missing her smile, her laugh...it ached, but as long as these assignments kept him in the field and away from the opportunity to ruin something so good, he'd play the coward.

"Earth to Duff." The t-shirt slipped off her shoulder, and, just like that, he was rock hard. "You froze."

"Sorry, I zoned out."

"Of course, you're probably exhausted." Her eyebrows knit together with concern.

"A bit."

"Anyway, I've got to go. My mom roped me into helping her clean out her attic."

"Good times. Gran seems to have me do that every time I'm back in Inverness."

"I bet. It should be relatively painless. Mom's not fond of taking trips down memory lane, so I shouldn't have to endure too long." Lovie ended with a soft laugh.

Duff caught himself staring again. God, she was gorgeous. He started mentally calculating the flight time from Marrakesh to Philadelphia.

"What?" She plucked something from her plate and popped it into her mouth to cover for the blush he knew was on her cheeks. It amazed him that she could be so confident yet still so insecure.

He wanted to tell her how the mere thought of her had kept him company at night. He wanted to tell her how she kept him going, through all of the travel. The banality of setting up and breaking down equipment, moving to the following location, and doing it all again.

Instead, he said, "nothin."

She smiled, slow and sweet, before disconnecting the call.

Duff was still thinking about that smile when he and Archie returned to their tent after dinner. As soon as he kicked off his boots, he dropped onto his cot and pulled out his phone.

I miss you.

She answered immediately, which made him both giddy and guilty.

I miss the way your eyes get all scrunchy when you're thinking.

Scrunchy?

Yeah, they crinkle at the edges.

" I swear," Archie said. "You're like a teenager."

"Don't be jealous, Arch."

The other man scoffed. "Not in the least. I'm just not used to seeing you like this."

Duff peeled his eyes away from his phone and looked up to where Archie was methodically repacking his rucksack. "Like what?"

Archie paused as if in thought. "Smitten."

Duff grinned. "That I am."

"Good for you."

Duff turned his attention back to his phone.

So, you miss my wrinkles. You're saying I'm old.

I'm saying you're cute.

Good save. I miss your shampoo.

LOL! My shampoo.

Can't walk by a bakery without sprouting wood.

OMG! You're so bad.

Just being honest. I also miss your laugh.

Awwww, I miss your smile.

And the way you look at me.

I like looking at you. I miss your face.

You just saw it.

Video isn't the same. Photos neither.

Truth. I miss your thighs, woman. They're so soft against my face when I'm tasting you. And I miss the sound you make when I—

Duff fired off a few more exchanges with Lovie and then put his phone down. His hands were shaking, and the fit of his cargo shorts was suddenly an issue. Across the tent, Archie happily blathered on about having lived in Scandinavia as he filled his flight case. Oblivious to the debauchery happening so close to him. A pause in his chatter prompted Duff to chime in. He needed something to take his mind off the soft, sexy woman on the other side of the ocean.

"You said you used to live in Finland?"

"Yeah. I'm sure I told you about it." Archie glanced over his shoulder, his thick, black hair wet and clinging to his face and neck. Duff couldn't wait to get out of this Moroccan heat.

"Ye might've. My brain's a little fried at the moment. This heat is brutal." It was more from texting with Lovie than anything else.

Archie swiped his arm across his forehead. "Well, enjoy it while you can. It'll be twenty-below when we get there."

"We, who?" Duff frowned. "I'll be in Bali for a week and then head to the States."

Archie eyed him. "You're not doing the Mount Ailigás gig?"

"Mount what?"

"Big meteorite landed in a remote area on the Finnish border? Freak storms are keeping people away?"

"Ben didn't offer it to me."

"Maybe because you mentioned something about needing more personal time." Archie shrugged, turning back to his packing. "If you want it, you should let him know before he offers the spot to someone else. Once that happens, you know how it goes."

"He might take me off his A-list."

"Ben doesn't like having to put together a team. Wants us on speed dial, ready and willing."

"I know." It had taken him four years to make his way onto their handler's go-to list, taking crap assignments until he'd worked his way up the food chain.

Duff's phone buzzed in his hand. It was Lovie.

Can't wait to see you!

Shit.

2

———

DEFINE "FRIENDS"

Duff gave Lovie a wicked smile before he slid down her body, taking the sheet with him. "I've missed you."

"Are you talking to my—?"

"Shhhhh. I'm busy here."

"Oh my God." Lovie laughed softly, but her back arched off the bed when Duff put his mouth on her for the second time since he showed up on her doorstep that evening. He made her feel so good, feel so much, she never wanted it to end. She fisted her hands in the sheets and rolled her hips for him.

It was all so confusing. The connection they had, the chemistry, the feeling of it being so *right* between them, none of it made sense. Lovie had done the calculations, and they'd spent a total of three weeks in the same space over the last nine or ten months. It should feel this good to be with someone.

Duff's mouth was doing wicked things to her body, but she needed those lips on hers right the hell now. "Come up here," she demanded.

He obeyed immediately, covering her with his hard body and going straight in for a kiss.

Lovie could taste herself on his tongue, and she moaned. Duff was the most sensual person she had ever known. She wanted to make him feel just as good, needed to feel him unravel.

"Need you in me," she husked. *One of these days*, she thought. They might not need a barrier between them.

For now, Duff wasted no time. He reached over to her nightstand and grabbed a condom, ripping it open and sheathing himself in a series of practiced moves that left her breathless.

When he notched himself at her entrance, Lovie lifted her hips to meet him, and he sank inside.

Duff rocked into her slowly, his face buried in the crook of her neck, and Lovie tried her best to wrap him up completely in her body. She kissed his shoulder, ran her hands down his back and over his ass, where she gave the firm globes a squeeze. She was rewarded with the sexiest groan against her skin.

They moved unhurriedly, with nothing but time stretching out in front of them. Lovie rocked with him in an endless rhythm that felt as old as the universe.

Duff was gentle, even as he was demanding, and easily the best lover she'd ever had. She didn't have to wonder if it was as good for him because he told her with words and his body.

Before she knew it, her climax overcame her. Stars burst behind her eyes, her heart fluttered wildly in her chest, and she wondered at the rightness of it all. When she came down, he wrapped his arms around her and settled her against his chest.

Lovie could feel the strong beat of his heart thumping against her temple as she tumbled into a dreamless sleep.

BATHED IN AN EARLY MORNING-AFTER GLOW, sunlight curled through the sheer curtains of the window and stretched down toward the bed where they lay entangled—her and Duff. Whatever they were.

She'd spent the night trying to hash it out in her mind and had landed on *let's see where it goes*. Lovie's head rested on one bicep of her warm, muscular, and nice-smelling...whatever Duff was to her.

There was absolutely nothing wrong with keeping things casual. But given their possessive hold on each other and the simmering desire that had been there since they first met, Lovie was fairly sure casual as in the rearview mirror. At least for her, it was. She liked him.

A lot.

Her leg lay trapped against the hard evidence of his arousal, and she was sure, given the way his hip settled between her thighs, he could feel her heat. The way his mouth kept brushing over hers, tasting and teasing — drawing her in and retreating on a groan...

Lovie turned to lie on her back, attempting to break whatever spell had been cast over them and return to reality.

"Hey you," came his soft protest and that *voice*, Holy mother of haggis. Deep and husky, it was as if Duff had traveled to the underworld and brought back all of its seductive parts. It was dark, dangerous, and sexy as, well, Hades.

"Hey, yourself."

Duff's soft breath tickled the sensitive skin behind her ear when he curled around her.

Lovie inhaled his spicy, woodsy scent. And his morning breath. Funny, she hadn't noticed it when his tongue was in her mouth. "We should probably brush our teeth," she whispered from behind her hand after she tested her own and found it equally unpleasant.

"Subtle." He chuckled, and she couldn't hold back her giggle.

"I'm nothing if not tactful."

Duff nipped at her earlobe. "You're sweet and gorgeous, and, ahh!" He yelped when she curled her feet around his. "Freezing! Christ, woman, you've got wee blocks of ice at the ends of your legs."

"And you're a walking furnace. Can you blame me?"

He laughed as he moved down her body, much as he had the night before. This time, he encased her frozen toes in his huge, hot hands. It was decadent, but now she missed having him all around her. Blue, almost iridescent eyes blinked up from the foot of the bed, full of mischief, as he rubbed her feet.

"Don't you dare," she warned.

He grinned, the devil. "I won't. I know how much you hate being tickled."

Hate was too weak a word. Lovie despised tickling. Tickling was right up there with nails on a blackboard, soft-boiled eggs, and Diddy in terms of things that creeped her out.

Duff paused, eyeing her now-curled toes. "But it is ever-so-tempting."

"And here I thought we were friends." A swarm of honeybees convened in her stomach, but she batted them away.

Duff's hands stilled as he looked up at her, a dark wave of his ebony hair falling across one eye. The six o'clock shadow dusting his chiseled jaw made him look like a pirate. Or a rake from one of her best friend's romance novels.

"Friends, eh?"

She couldn't help but grin at him.

"What?" He returned it, always ready to share a joke.

"Nothing, you just look like a pirate." Duff winced, and she laughed. "More Jack Sparrow than Captain Hook, don't worry."

"Pfft. At least make me a Scottish pirate." Duff laughed and sat up, sweeping his hair back from his all-too-expressive eyes. There was humor in them, but also something else. Something that tugged at her core, twisting her belly into intricate knots.

"Is that what you want?" he asked almost shyly. "To be, uh, friends?"

Lovie pulled herself up to rest on her elbows, wanting to keep him in her sight. Her mind went blank as her gaze raked over his glorious cotton-clad chest, down and down his rippling abdomen to where she knew a dark trail of silky hair led to the treasure below his waistband.

"It's hard to want more than that when we have so little time together." She tried to keep her voice even, but Lovie's stomach was doing somersaults inside. "Even now, our time has been cut in half because you have an unplanned assignment. I'm not complaining," she added quickly.

"You have every right to complain. And we'll get more time

together soon." He leveled her with that aqua gaze that had the annoying ability to turn her insides to mush. "I promise."

They'd talked over a late dinner. Well, Lovie had talked. Duff had mostly apologized and apologized. And had kept apologizing. It had gotten a little old, but she'd tried to keep the annoyance out of her voice when she reassured him that all was forgiven. She never wanted to get between him and his work.

"It's fine." Lovie's words slurred as Duff began to massage her calves.

His hands were warm and slightly calloused. They felt good. Too good. She couldn't hold back the tiny moan that left her throat.

"That nice?" A wicked glint entered his gaze, and his fingers dug deeper into her flesh.

Lovie let her head drop back. The bed shifted with Duff's weight as he knelt between her legs, using his thighs to push hers apart.

"So nice."

"Good." His hands moved up, kneading her muscles into submission. It was a pleasure bordering on the edge of discomfort but, so worth it.

"You enjoy giving massages?" Lovie didn't even try to fight the breathiness of her words. How could she be expected to keep her wits about her when he touched her like this?

"Only to certain people," came his low response.

Lovie's hips had rotated a few degrees before she caught them. She inhaled slowly and deeply, trying to rein in her body's response to the man.

"Come here."

Duff released Lovie's legs and grabbed her hands, pulling her into a sitting position. He motioned her to the edge of the bed, and she willingly obeyed.

His heat once again surrounded her. His scent, male, and spice, filled the air around them. Firm hands landed on her shoulders, and those nimble fingers pressed into them. Lovie dropped her chin to her chest in surrender.

Duff worked her muscles like a pro, and Lovie wondered if he'd ever trained as a masseur.

"You're so tense, love." Ah, God, and now that voice was right in her ear again, working its way into her brain and migrating to parts south.

Lovie shivered at the endearment. Tense? That was one word for it. She was wound tighter than a spool of thread. It was too much. His voice, his touch, his everything. Too much.

"When your hands are on me, it's hard to wrap my head around how much I'll miss you when you go." Lovie's admission surprised even herself.

Duff rested his palms on her shoulders. His thumbs glided up and down the nape of her neck, and Lovie could feel the slight tremble in his hands. He seemed just as wrapped up in this as she was.

"What are we doing?"

Duff stilled. "We're...enjoying each other's company. Aren't we?"

"Company," Lovie repeated the word. It tasted so generic on her tongue.

Duff sighed and moved to sit next to her outstretched leg. One hand caressed her shin, causing goosebumps to erupt again under the sleep shirt she'd pulled on during the night.

"We have a rare connection here, I think," he began slowly, ducking his head to peer at her under her no-doubt unruly hair. "It's an unusual bond, agreed? Unusual for me, at least. Can't speak for you."

Lovie nodded. "Agreed. It's definitely different."

Her heart pounded against her ribcage, and the breath halted in her lungs, awaiting the *but* she heard in his tone. He gestured with his free hand as if trying to pluck the words from the air.

"I've never clicked with anyone like this." He brushed a stray curl out of her eye. "I mean that, Lovie. I'm not just talking shite. You're important to me."

At least he didn't say *special*. Lovie would have kicked him. She knew exactly what he meant about their connection. She felt it, too, and had from their very first conversation. Had that only been nine months ago? Geez.

"You're important to me too, Duff."

His answering smile was one of relief and gratitude. "I'm so glad for that 'cause I kinda need you in my life. Nothing worse than findin' a treasure and then losin' it."

Lovie smiled and nudged his shoulder. "Well, regardless. You're stuck with me."

"Aye, and you're stuck with me, but I'm a realist. Yeah? This... thing we have might not go where we might want it to go." Regret flashed behind his eyes, its answer a squeeze in Lovie's chest.

"I know. I live here, and you travel ninety-nine percent of the time."

"As you said, I can't even promise when we'll see one another," Duff lamented.

"I know, Duff." She knew it, and she hated it. Why hadn't they invented teleporters already? Wasn't this the twenty-first century, dammit?

"Am I being an arsehole?" His hand had moved up her leg, his touches again softening into caresses.

No matter what words came from his gorgeous lips, his desire for her was evident in the tightness around his eyes. The slight flare of his nostrils. The tongue that toyed with the corner of his mouth.

Lovie fought the urge to glance down at his zipper, afraid she'd act on what she'd undoubtedly find. She stretched her leg out further, just a bit, eager for more contact.

He didn't disappoint.

But it was more than desire. He got her, and she thought she understood what drove him. They were in tune with one another. Duff was loyal, caring, smart, funny, and creative. He was everything she might want in a partner. She didn't know if he *wanted* that. A partnership, relationship, whatever.

"You're not an arsehole. You're just being practical, and I'm nothing if not a pragmatist." Lovie flopped back onto the bed, exhausted from the emotional roller coaster. "Being an adult sucks."

Duff stretched his long body across the mattress and rested his head on her hip. He threw one arm across her belly, his thumb skimming the bare skin of her arm. The pressure of that small touch was maddening, and her skin sang in that one little spot.

"I don't disagree with that," he said, chuckling. "Still, I think this could go a lot of places. We're always going to be close. I can feel it."

Lovie thought so, too. No matter what happened, she had her parents, Jo, and now Duff. It was a small consolation nonetheless. What more could they be if they allowed it?

"So...we're friends?" Lovie wove her fingers into his ebony hair. Why, oh, why did it have to be so thick, and wavy, and so damn yummy?

"More than friends, Lovie luv." He tightened the arm around her waist, and she felt claimed. "Much, much more."

Hmm. How much?

"Friends with benefits?" The joke fell flat as it left her mouth. She'd always loathed that term. She also despised the fact that she needed his hands on her and hoped he couldn't hear the desperation in her voice.

"Such bullshit," he gruffed, pulling her closer still. "Some arsehole with commitment issues invented that to get shagged, I'm sure of it."

"That's harsh." Lovie snorted. "So, we're friends without benefits?"

Duff tilted his head, and the heat in his gaze stole her breath.

Lovie offered him a shaky smile, but he didn't return it. How he could look at her, as if he could see straight down into the well of her deepest desires, should have been impossible. And yet, there he was doing just that.

"What?" She averted her eyes, the need to mask his effect on her imperative. "I'm only kidding."

Duff reached up and tilted her chin, forcing her to meet his eyes. Twin oceans that swam with possibilities.

"I don't know what the future holds, but I cannae pretend I don't want you. And I don't mean just physically, though that...I do."

Lovie watched the movement of his throat as he swallowed hard. She nearly moaned when his tongue darted out to lick his bottom lip. Her nipples had sharpened into tiny daggers behind the thin cotton of her tank top, and she cursed herself for not putting on a bra the night before.

The corner of Duff's mouth ticked up in recognition, his thumb moving across her cheek in slow, languid strokes. "You can't pretend either."

"Never said I could." She couldn't mask the huskiness in her voice. *Or that I want to.* Lovie kept those words in the back of her throat.

Duff's hand fell from her face, and she immediately missed the contact. He nodded toward her bathroom.

"I need to get going." He leaned up to press a quick, hard kiss to her cheek.

"Okay."

Their gazes locked for long moments, each passing second making it much harder for her to take a steady breath. Duff's expression was pure hunger, and she felt every beat of her pounding heart between her thighs. Heat prickled across her skin like marching fire ants.

Inhaling deeply, Duff groaned and cursed under his breath. He sat up, putting distance between them that Lovie loathed. She wasn't sure how she'd handle thousands of miles and continents between them if they were really together. Maybe being friends was for the best.

Still, Lovie watched, rapt, as he slid off the bed. He stretched to his full height and then some.

"Right." He rubbed one hand over his abs and across the flat plane of his stomach as he yawned, his boxer briefs only accentuating the tight curves of his ass as he walked away. Was he fucking kidding? "I'll be quick."

Gods, he was sexy, and Lovie wanted him—again—so much her mouth watered.

Duff wanted her, too. Badly, by the looks of it. She'd caught a glimpse of his erection before he'd turned to go. She'd seen the naked desire in his eyes. Would they ever be able to walk away from this kind of chemistry?

Lovie followed Duff into the bathroom before she could talk herself out of it.

Surprised eyes met hers in the mirror, but Duff smiled around his toothbrush when she joined him, brushing her teeth silently at his side. After she had rinsed, she caught his gaze in the mirror. He'd been watching her. No, Duff's eyes had been consuming her. Drinking her in. Lovie's body thrummed, just from the longing in his expression. God, she felt that hunger down to her toes.

Lovie crossed to the standing shower and opened the glass door. Reaching inside, she started the water, adjusting the temperature to her liking. She hooked her thumbs into the waistband of her pajama bottoms, pushed them over her hips, and let them drop to her feet before stepping out of them. Her T-shirt was next. With her back to Duff, she crossed her arms and lifted the soft material over her head. It dropped soundlessly to the marble floor.

"Lovie."

The word was a low, rolling thunder of a warning, but Lovie ignored it. She could practically feel his eyes burning into her. She hooked her thumbs into the elastic of her undies and pushed them down, making sure to bend over and give Duff a nice view of her bare ass. It was unfair. Lovie knew it, and she just didn't care. She wanted him, he wanted her, and they were whole-ass adults.

Lovie opened the shower door and stepped inside. When she moved under the spray, she heard the clatter of something falling to the floor.

"Fuck." It was a long, dragged-out whisper of a word.

Lovie smiled but didn't turn to look at him. "Everything okay?"

"You are playing a dangerous game."

Gloriously warm water splashed across her body, dotting every curve, and Lovie turned to face him. She ran her hands along the same paths the water took and watched as his jaw bunched. His gaze was pure fire.

"Jesus," he groaned. "You're not making this easy."

She wasn't trying to make it easy. And maybe it wasn't fair, but what was that saying about love and war?

"Come here." She crooked one finger, beckoning him.

"I'm going to miss my flight." Duff seemed conflicted but also seriously turned on. *So hot.* And despite his apparent reluctance, he stalked forward, his hand at his waist. He yanked down his briefs, his eyes on hers.

"What do you think you're doing?" His voice had dropped into a growl, and the sound of it sent shivers up Lovie's spine.

Duff had given her a taste, and she wasn't ready to let go again. Not yet. She wanted to squeeze every second of that something out of these waning moments that she could.

Lovie widened the door and opened her arms. "I'm sure there's a later flight you can catch." She offered him a hand and pulled him inside when he took it. "I'm not quite done with you yet."

3

WHO ARE WE KIDDING?

Something about the thrill of a tough assignment spiked Duff's adrenaline. He'd never thought of himself as a thrill junkie, but he had to admit, it did turn him on. Throughout his career, Duff has worked through a whole season on Planet Earth. Deserts, oceans, mountains, and rainforests, but this was the first time he'd spent any length of time in such inhospitable cold. It sucked.

Minus thirty-eight degrees Celsius might sound chilly in a forecast, but it was nothing compared to the real thing. It was a biting cold that gnawed on his bones and froze the vapor of his breath as it left his nose. Any more layers of clothing, and he wouldn't be able to move his limbs. His leather gloves were lined with Smart Wool, which helped, but not much. Even they would have to come off when it came time to shoot.

"Hey, Scotland, where do you want the reflectors set up?" Archie asked. Born in Honolulu, he was in constant motion, shifting from one foot to the next to stave off the cold. Duff had been teasing him about his inability to handle the subzero temps since they'd landed in Lakselv.

As they whirled a few hundred feet above a vast and forbidding tundra, buzzers sounding out in alarm all around them, Duff's immediate worry wasn't about the cold.

His first thought was that he was a knobhead for trusting a few pitifully thin panels of carbon fiber to keep them safe, especially in the hands of a pilot whose veins were filled with more vodka than blood. It was a goddamned deathtrap, and now they were going to crash and burn in a ball of fire and ice.

His second thought was that he should have used the loo. He really had to go, and if he was going to die, he didn't want his body to be found in a puddle of frozen piss. Never mind that it would make a great shot.

His third thought was Lovie. And his fourth. And every thought after. What was he doing? Thirty-six hours ago, he'd been safe and warm in her arms, his heart trying to beat itself out of his chest and stay with her. He should have listened to it for a change.

Instead, he'd let his pragmatic mind lead him into this death trap. And for what?

This was probably the end for him. He'd miss her smile, her laugh, the way she smelled. The way she felt the last time he slid inside her—soft, warm, and welcoming. The grace she afforded him to follow his dream. A dream that was turning into a nightmare.

Lovie expected to meet him online at six her time. He couldn't let anything keep him from that. It's not that he'd never missed a meet-up. God knows he'd done that plenty. But if he missed this one... If he died out there, right then, she'd spend days thinking that he'd dropped out of contact again, only to learn that he was truly gone this time. It would be a sucker punch.

He couldn't let that happen.

The pilot wrestled with the controls as they spun in what seemed like slow motion.

"Did you send out a mayday?" Duff asked him.

"*Mitä*?" The man grimaced as another alarm sounded from the control board.

"A mayday call. An emergency...*fuck*." He turned to Archie. "What's the Finnish word for mayday?"

Archie shook his head violently, eyes wild. "I thought mayday was universal."

There was a loud crunch before everything went dark.

When Duff came-to, frigid air slapped him in the face, squeezing tears from his eyes. A low green light was the only thing holding off the pitch black. Duff thought he heard two distinct breathing patterns, one even and one...sort of wet sounding.

"Archie?" His throat felt raw. No one answered.

Duff's chattering teeth made speaking difficult, and he'd lost feeling in places that had never seen the light of day. He felt more like an ice sculpture than a human being. A mental inventory didn't reveal anything more than stiffness and a few bruises. He felt underneath his seat for his backpack and pulled it up onto his lap.

Minus twenty-nine degrees Celsius had sounded cold, but Duff learned there was a world of difference between knowing it and feeling it. The weather report had warned of a deep mass of arctic air settling over the region. The pilot had turned his first offer down, but money was a universal language. Duff doubled his offer, and the man gleefully accepted. The woman at the general store shook her head as she rang up his provisional purchases.

"I would not fly today in this." She'd smiled and shook her head. Duff and his partner had shrugged her off. What was a little chilly air when they had such a thrilling assignment? The pay was astronomical for so short a gig.

Only now, they were stuck, quite literally, on thin ice.

But the northern lights were stunning, and the pilot quietly snored. Asleep after all of this, the fucker.

"You okay, Scotland?"

Thank heavens. "M'fine. How many hours 'til daybreak?"

"Three. And then they'll try the rescue. Our pilot drifted off after sending the mayday and receiving the instruction to wait until the wind advisory subsided."

"Fuck me." Duff shifted and located the emergency thermal blanket in his kit.

Archie pulled his own blanket over him. "You flaking out already? It's only two o'clock."

"Shut up. Ye already know I'm no' built for this."

"Dude, no one is built for this."

"Aye, but you aren't even shivering."

"That's because I'm frozen solid." Archie's hearty laugh, punctuated by clouds of cold exhalation, morphed into a stuttering cough. He pulled the blanket up to his chin as his body shook. After a moment, he quieted, much to Duff's relief. The pilot had taken the brunt of the impact but seemed oblivious to his pain and the cold.

Duff couldn't sleep, so he kept watch. The light of the SOS beacon cast an eerie glow on an already eerie setting. Black on black on green, while the occasional ribbon of iridescent light shimmered in the sky above. He fished out his point-and-shoot camera, removing his glove long enough to take a few shots to share with Lovie.

He needed to get back to her, needed to tell her—to confess—what he wanted. What he's wanted all along.

I love her. I love the fuck out of her, and I might expire out here on this ice. She'd never know.

Fuck that.

Lovie blinked a few times after she opened the door, sure she was hallucinating. Duff couldn't possibly be back again so soon. She stood there, her weekend bag in hand, and stared at him.

"Hi," he said weakly.

Damn.

Lovie hated the quiver she got in his stomach from a single word from Duff's mouth. She was angry, dammit. He'd not only shortened his last stay and canceled all their plans, but now he'd added a surprise visit to her list of 'things good guys don't do.'

But his face.

And his...arm. Concern washed away every other emotion, and Lovie moved toward him. "What happened?"

He tried to evade her touch but she wasn't having that. "Were you off somewhere?"

"Duff..."

He hesitated. It was only a split second, and anybody else might not have noticed, but Lovie did. "I...fell out of a tree."

"A tree?" She ghosted her fingers over the plastic cast that encased his right arm from elbow to fingers. "What were you doing in a tree?"

He ducked his head, rubbing the back of his neck with his good arm. "Ah, er...tryin' to get down?"

Lovie gave him a wordless *no-shit Sherlock* and resumed her examination. The visible tips of his fingers were seven different shades of black and blue. It looked painful. He stiffened when she touched the index finger, confirming her summation.

"There was a helicopter... It's a long story."

"Did they give you anything for the pain?"

"Yah, and I'm due for one. Could I trouble you for some water?"

The concern Lovie felt kicked her into caretaker mode. She ushered him over to the couch before hustling into the kitchen for a bottle of spring water. She returned to find Duff resting against the cushions, head back and eyes closed. If it weren't for the tightness at the corners of his mouth and eyes, she wouldn't have known he was in pain. He clearly was. And she wanted answers, but perhaps now wasn't the time to dig for them.

"Here."

Duff's eyes snapped open as he sat forward. "Ta."

Lovie watched as he pulled a small white envelope from his pocket, emptied a small orange pill onto her coffee table, and replaced it. He popped the pill and chased it with the water, eyes tight and mouth set in a grimace. After a beat, he opened his eyes and smiled, mouth only.

"Thanks for removing the cap."

"I figured it would be a challenge in your current state."

He offered a half-laugh. The silence between them was sodden like a rain-soaked meadow. Any misstep and they'd end up covered in muck, she knew, but she still had to ask.

"What happened?"

Duff sighed and sat back. "We went up when we should have stayed down. Helicopter. Nothing to worry about, I'm fine. Or, I will be."

Something was up, but Lovie decided not to press. His eyes were drooping, probably from a combination of the travel and the meds they'd given him for the pain.

"When did you get back to the States?"

"Yesterday. I had to take care of some business in New York, and then I took the train down this morning." He met her eyes. "I probably should have called."

"You think?" Lovie's anger seeped back in.

"I'm sorry." He was all hard lines and soft eyes and lips that stole her reason. Sorry never looked so good.

Duff winced as he tried to remove his jacket. Lovie thought twice about helping him, but her sympathy won out. Together, they maneuvered the warm leather off, avoiding the cast altogether. Duff tossed it onto the couch beside him.

"Thank you. Looks like you were heading out."

"Oh, I..." It was Lovie's turn to fidget. "Jo and I were going to check into a resort for the weekend. There's a spa..." she trailed off.

"Oh, shit." Duff sat up straighter. "I'm so sorry, I should go."

Lovie put her hand on his uninjured arm. "No rush. I was going to throw my suitcase in the car. She won't be back from work for a while."

Silence formed between them, but it was clear that Duff had something to say.

"What's on your mind?" she asked, unable to stop herself.

Duff raised his eyes to hers, a storm brewing behind them. "There's something I've been wanting to tell ye, but I... I canna find the right words."

She sighed and removed her hand from his arm. This was it, then. "Duff, I get it. And to be honest, it's been hard for me, too."

"No, I—"

"It's okay. Really, it's fine." She tried to give him a smile, but it felt more like a grimace. She was an adult. She could handle this like an adult. It wasn't like they were ever *together*-together. "Like you said, we'll always be friends. We have a connection. Right?"

He nodded slowly, but a frown creased his brow. "Is that what you want, Lovie?"

"We can't always get what we want."

"That's evasive." He arched a brow.

Lovie shrugged. "Still true."

"How about," he began, "I tell you what I want, and you tell me if it's possible."

Lovie sank back into the couch cushions, needing something to ground her because she was beginning to think she had the wrong end of the stick. One way or another.

"Alright, then. Tell me what you want."

He took a deep breath, wincing slightly as he shifted on the sofa to face her.

"I want to stop. I… Look, for the last ten years, I've been in motion. Always on the go, ye ken? Other than me Gran, I've not known what home feels like. And even with her, Inverness hasna been a home to me for a long time. But with you…"

He searched her eyes.

"With me?" Lovie reached out, and Duff took her hand in his. It was warm and strong, and he gripped her tightly.

"From the moment we met, yeah? There was *something*, and it's only gotten bigger. Stronger. Ten days, ten weeks, ten months, it doesna matter. You got me."

"Did I?" Lovie's insides quivered as she bit back her smile. He was adorably flustered and so obviously gone for her. How had she missed that? Something inside her unwound and relaxed.

He exhaled slowly. "I'm in love with you."

"Good."

He huffed out a surprised laugh. "Good?"

Lovie lifted his arm and snuggled into his side, smiling broadly. "I mean, I didn't want to be the only one who'd lost the plot, as you say."

Duff rested his chin atop her head. "Definitely not. So, I was thinking… When you return from your trip, I could visit ye for a while."

"No."

"No?"

"No, you'll stay here while Jo and I go. It's only for the weekend, and then we'll be back."

He moved to look down at her. "You want me to stay in yer flat while you're away? Will Jo be okay with it?"

"Please," Lovie said, laughing. "No one ships us harder than that girl. She'll be thrilled. And I'll owe her fifty bucks."

"Did you make a bet over me?" His mouth curved into a grin.

"Don't ask." Lovie reached up and ran a hand through his hair, loving the way he curled into her touch. "How long of a visit are we talking about this time? Until you're all healed up?"

Duff glanced down at his arm. "Oh, this'll be fine in a day or two. No, I was thinking…until I find a place of me own."

Lovie sat up so fast she jostled Duff's injured arm.

"Ow, fuck."

"Yikes, I'm so sorry." She fussed over him. "What can I do?"

Laughing, Duff waved her off. "Jes *don't* do *that*."

"God, right. Sorry. You said… Well, I thought you said you were going to look for your own place. Here? In Philly?"

He nodded, grinning shyly. "It seems like the best way to see you every day."

"Ah, I see." Lovie bit her lip. "Logical, for now. The *best* way would probably be to live together, but that seems too soon."

The smile he gave her stole her breath. "A bit, but not by much."

The buzzer rang, startling them both.

"That'll be Jo waiting for me downstairs."

"You go enjoy your girls' weekend, and I'll be here when you get home."

She kissed him, slow and deep. "Home. I like the way you say that."

"I like saying it when it comes to you."

DUFF STRETCHED out on the couch and took a deep breath. Being in Lovie's space was strange without her with him, but it still felt right. He liked the idea of waiting for her. Felt it was only right that he take a turn doing that.

The front door swung open, and an out-of-breath Jo stumbled through it.

"Hey, you!"

Sitting up, Duff smiled. "Hi yourself! Did you forget something?"

"I totally forgot that I have a dentist appointment tomorrow." She grinned widely.

"On a Saturday?"

"Yep!" She dragged her suitcase through the door. It was huge for a trip that was only supposed to be for two days. "So, I can't possibly go to the luxurious mountain resort with my bestie this weekend. I wonder if you might be able to take my place?"

"Jo, you don't havta—?

"Oh, yes. I do. This yours?" She grabbed his duffle from the floor. When he nodded, she gestured toward the door. "Get off your ass, mister, and don't keep our girl waiting any longer. It's been long enough, hasn't it?"

Duff got to his feet and took the bag from her. "Far too long."

He took the stairs two at a time and pushed through the door to the sidewalk, pausing when he saw Lovie leaning against the car. Her hair ruffled in the wind as she smiled at him.

"Well? Are you coming?"

Striding over to her, Duff knew he would follow this woman anywhere. "I'm all yours."

DUFF'S GRAN'S CRANACHAN RECIPE

A creamy, dreamy dessert that melts in your mouth, Cranachan has layers of sweet berries, crunchy oatmeal, and silky-smooth whipped cream, all kissed with a hint of smoky whisky and a drizzle of honey.

The origin of the word cranachan in Scots Gaelic means "churn." Sometimes the dessert is referred to as "crowdie," as the cheese of the same name was sometimes used instead of the whipped cream in this recipe. Whatever you call it, there's a taste of the Scottish Highlands in every spoonful!

Cranachan is perfect for any celebration, but especially Christmas, Hogmanay, or your Burns Night supper.

Prep Time: 5 mins

Cook Time: 10 mins

Chill Time: 60 mins

Total: 75 mins

Serves 6

Ingredients:

2 cups/475ml heavy cream

1 ½ cups raspberries (Scottish if you can find them.) Strawberries also work

¼ cup rolled oats

A healthy dram of your favourite whisky (about 3 tablespoons) (optional)

1 tablespoon of quality honey

Walker's Shortbread for garnish. Crushed meringues may also be used.

To Make:

• Place a large heavy-bottomed skillet over medium-high heat until hot, but not smoking.

• Add the oats and stir constantly, toasting them until they have a light, nutty smell and start to change color, about 3 minutes. (Don't leave the oats unattended or they might burn.) Remove immediately from the pan.

• Place the 1 1/4 cup berries in a food processor. (Save the remaining ¼ for garnish.) Pulse to create a thick purée but do not over-blend it. Lumps are okay for this dish.

• In the bowl of a stand mixer fitted with the whisk attachment, whisk together the heavy cream along with the 3 tablespoons malt whisky (optional) to form firm peaks, about 3 minutes. Alternatively, use a hand-held electric mixer. Do not overwhip.

• Fold in the honey.

• Add in the cooled oats and berry purée.

• Gently fold all together and spoon into glasses. Garnish the top with the rest of the fresh raspberries and a shortbread biscuit or bits of crumbled meringue.

• Pour yourself another dram of whiskey to sip and enjoy your Cranachan!

LOVIE'S SPICED APPLE SPRITZ

This cocktail is refreshing and sophisticated, combining the warmth of Scotch with the crispness of apple and the effervescence of sparkling wine. Perfect for cozy winter nights in front of the fire, but also great year-round.

Ingredients:

1 ounce Scotch (whiskey or rye will substitute)

1 ½ ounces Apple Cider

2 ½ ounces Sparkling Wine

½ ounce Simple Syrup (or 1 tbsp Honey)

Cinnamon to taste

Apple slices for garnish

Ice

Directions:

Pour the whisky, cider, and simple syrup into a highball glass.

Sprinkle with cinnamon, add ice, and stir to combine until well chilled.

Top with sparkling wine, garnish with apple slices, and cinnamon.

Serve immediately.

NOTE: To make a non-alcoholic version, substitute 4 ounces of sparkling apple cider for the apple cider and the sparkling wine in the recipe. If you don't have sparkling cider, combine 2 ounces of apple juice/cider with 2 ounces of sparkling water.

ACKNOWLEDGMENTS

Thank you to my team at Milk N Cookies for always having my back, especially Ann Jones.

Huge thanks to my family for always talking me up wherever they go.

Heartfelt thanks to all my readers: the ones who have been there since day one, and the ones who only recently joined the Xioverse. I couldn't do any of this without you.

All my love forever to Mr. X who puts up with the voices in my head and cheers on all my mad ideas.

ALSO BY XIO AXELROD

The Lillys

The Girl with Stars in Her Eyes

Girls with Bad Reputations

Plays and Players

Love on the Byline

Frankie and Johnny

When Frankie Meets Johnny

Frankie and Johnny: Let the Music Play

Falling Stars

Falling Stars

Starlight

Camden

Fast Forward

The Warm Up

ABOUT THE AUTHOR

Xio Axelrod [she/her] is a USA Today bestselling author. She writes different flavors of contemporary fiction, romance, and what she likes to call, "strange, twisted tales."

Xio grew up in the recording industry and began performing at a very young age. A completely unapologetic, badge-wearing, fic-writing fangirl, Xio finds inspiration in everything around her. From her quirky neighbors to the lyrics of whatever song she currently has on repeat, to the latest clips from her favorite TV series, SKAM, Xio weaves her passions into her books.

(And if you're curious about SKAM, ask her about it. Just be prepared to settle in for the long haul.)

When she isn't working on the next story, Xio can be found behind a microphone in a studio, writing songs in her bedroom-turned-recording-booth, or occasionally performing under a different, not-so-secret name.

She lives in complete denial of the last five minutes of Buffy with one very patient, full-time, indoor husband, and several part-time, supremely pampered, outdoor cats.

For all the latest news, click here!

9 781735 233772